LYNNE KELLY

CHAINED

MARGARET FERGUSON BOOKS
FARRAR STRAUS GIROUX
NEW YORK

Farrar Straus Giroux Books for Young Readers
175 Fifth Avenue, New York 10010

Printed in the United States of America
by RR Donnelley & Sons Company, Harrisonburg, Virginia
Designed by Jay Colvin
First edition, 2012
3   5   7   9   10   8   6   4

mackids.com

Library of Congress Cataloging-in-Publication Data
Kelly, Lynne, 1969–
    Chained / Lynne Kelly. — 1st ed.
        p.   cm.
    Summary: To work off a family debt, ten-year-old Hastin
leaves his desert village in India to work as a circus elephant
keeper but many challenges await him, including trying to keep
Nandita, a sweet elephant, safe from the cruel circus owner.
    ISBN 978-0-374-31237-4 (hardcover)
    ISBN 978-0-374-31250-3 (e-book)
    [1. Conduct of life—Fiction.   2. Elephants—Fiction.
3. Animals—Treatment—Fiction.   4. Circus—Fiction.
5. Child labor—Fiction.   6. India—Fiction.]   I. Title.

PZ7.K29639Ch 2012
[Fic]—dc23

                                                    2011031767

To my parents, who gave me books,
and to Samantha, for being my someone to read to

CHAINED

1

*An entire herd of elephants will care for a member
that falls ill.*

        —From *Care of Jungle Elephants* by Tin San Bo

The flood left, but the fever stayed.

    I sit on the floor of our hut and hold a cold wash-cloth to Chanda's forehead. My mother boils another pot of basil tea on our village's clay stove in the court-yard. Voices of our neighbors gathered around her flow through the open door of our home.

"Here—papaya juice with honey."

"Have you tried raisins with ginger? Boil them together and have her drink the liquid."

"Take these onions, Parvati. When my son had a fever, I made him onion broth."

September marked the end of monsoon season, but an

October rain flooded the river near our village last week. We all worried about the humming of mosquitoes that followed the water. Sometimes mosquitoes carry fever.

Sometimes the fever is stronger than a cold washcloth and basil tea and onions.

One of the fever-mosquitoes must have bitten my little sister, because she's been sick for five days. She is too tired to get up from her blanket. She does not want to eat or drink, not even fresh milk mixed with sugar.

Our mother enters the hut, holding a tea glass and a wooden bowl. She sets the tea glass next to me and kneels on the other side of Chanda.

"Neera made you papaya juice with honey. This will help you feel better."

She puts one hand behind Chanda's head and brings the bowl to her lips. Carefully she pours some papaya juice into Chanda's mouth.

"My head hurts, Amma."

"One more sip." She gives her another taste, then sets the bowl down and lowers Chanda's head to the blanket.

"Should we take her to a doctor, Amma?" I whisper.

She does not answer.

"I know we have no money, but . . ." Ever since Baba died last year, I feel like my family is sliding down a hill of sand, clawing and grabbing for anything to hang on to.

"She will get better, Hastin," Amma says, but her eyes do not leave Chanda's face. "The fever will break with the next glass of tea, or with another good night's sleep. And everyone is praying she will get well," she adds.

They pray she will get well but speak like she will not.

I don't tell Amma about the neighbor who whispered to her husband last night as they left our hut. "How sad for Parvati," she had said. "First her husband, and now to lose her little girl . . ." The man quieted his wife after he glanced back at me.

"Keep giving her the juice and the tea. While I'm making dinner I'll boil some onions for broth." Amma touches Chanda's face and forces a smile. "She is getting better, don't you think?"

No, I don't. I want to grab Amma's shoulders and shake her and yell, *Can't you see she's getting worse? Do something! Make her better!* But she has some hope left and I don't want to take it away.

She stands and hurries back to the courtyard.

Next to me, a fire burns in a mud-plastered bucket. A metal grill lies across the top of it. I set the tea glass on the grill so the fire will keep it warm. Once again, I dip the washcloth into a bowl of cold water, then place it across Chanda's forehead. Her chest moves up and down as she sleeps.

My stomach growls when I smell the roti dough baking in the clay oven outside.

I hope we will eat dinner soon—the flatbread tastes best when I pour the buttermilk on while it is still hot. Maybe we will even have beans tonight.

The sun dips lower in the sky, and the hut grows dark. Too early to light the lamp, though. From the wooden trunk that holds my belongings, I grab the ball Amma made me from fabric scraps and take it outside. Amma sits in front of the courtyard stove, covering her face with the end of her sari as gray smoke billows toward her.

Raj runs to me with his tail wagging. Chanda and I found him one day, drinking from the puddle around the water pump. He was so thin we could see his ribs beneath his sand-colored fur.

Amma wouldn't let us keep him. "We don't need one more mouth to feed!" she'd said when we asked her. But Raj doesn't have anyone else. When Amma isn't watching, Chanda and I bring him some of our dinner or a cup of milk. We shrug and try to look puzzled when she asks, "Why is that dog always following you around?"

Amma saw me petting Raj last week after I gave him a bite of roti. "The dog is getting fatter since you found him," she said, but I think she smiled a little.

From the doorway I throw the ball over and over again as far as I can, and Raj chases it and brings it back to me. He could play this game all day long.

"Amma?"

I let the ball drop to the ground and turn toward Chanda's voice. I rush into the house and kneel next to her, then brush back the wet strands of hair matted against her face. Raj follows me into the hut and nudges me with the ball before setting it down next to me.

"Chanda, are you feeling better?" Raj licks her face as I take the tea glass from the grill of the bucket fire. "Here, have some more tea."

She pushes the glass away.

"Do you want to rest in your playhouse?" I ask her. Chanda's always asking me to set up her playhouse for her. It's her favorite place to play with her doll or listen to stories I tell her.

She doesn't answer, but I grab two wooden trunks anyway and drag them across the floor. Then I set one near her head and one at her feet. From Amma's trunk I grab a purple sari, Chanda's favorite color, and drape it across the trunks to make a ceiling. The lamp I light shines through the fabric and makes a sunset on the wall.

Now and then I place a hand behind Chanda's head to help her take a drink. Finally she tilts the tea glass against her mouth for the last sip, then hands me the empty glass. I lean over to kiss her forehead. Still warm, but maybe not as burning hot as before. I run to the courtyard to tell Amma.

Just as I start to fall asleep that night I dream that Baba is playing catch with me and Raj. But then Chanda's voice pulls me away.

"Hastin, it's too hot."

I open my eyes and turn toward Chanda, where she lies on her blanket.

"I'm awake, what is it?" I ask. After Baba died, Chanda started having nightmares. When that happens I hold her hand until she falls asleep again. "Did you have a bad dream?"

"I'm burning up."

I crawl to her and touch her forehead, then hurry over to my mother.

"Amma, wake up!"

"What is it, Hastin? I am so tired," she says.

"It's Chanda."

Amma sits up and flings off her blanket.

"What's wrong?" She races to Chanda and puts her hand on her cheek before I can answer. "Her fever is worse than before!" Amma lights a lamp from a nearby shelf. The lamplight reveals spots of red covering Chanda's face and hands. *Oh, please, no . . .*

We have seen others break out in red spots after a bite from a fever-mosquito. If they get to the doctor in time, sometimes they get well and come back. Sometimes.

"What can we do, Amma?" I ask.

She picks up Chanda, limp like a doll in her arms. "I will take her to Amar's and ask him for a ride to the hospital."

"I want to go with you."

"No, stay here and take care of things. I'll be back as soon as I can." She carries Chanda across the courtyard to our neighbor Amar's house. He owns a rickshaw, so he can get them to the hospital in the city faster than anyone else.

"Amma, will she be all right?" I wait for her to give me some hope to cling to, to tell me again, *She will get better.*

She stops and turns to me. "I don't know, Hastin. All we can do is pray."

2

If necessary for survival, a herd divides itself into two.
   —From *Care of Jungle Elephants* by Tin San Bo

From the doorway I watch Amar pedal out of sight with my whole world in the back of his rickshaw.

Inside the hut, I place the lamp next to the wooden figure of Ganesh. Of all the carvings my father made, this one of the elephant-headed god is what we have left. One by one we have sold the others, when Amma has shaken the last grains of rice from the bag and doesn't have enough sewing work to buy more. But we hold on to Ganesh. He is the remover of obstacles, and we need him.

"Glory to you, O Lord Ganesh, son of goddess Parvati and the great god Shiv." *Chanda's head was so hot.*

"Single-tusk kind lord with four arms, with the mark on your forehead, riding your mouse." *She has to be all right.*

Silently I continue: *I'm sorry. I hope you will not mind if I just ask for what I want. Chanda needs to get well, and we need a way to pay the hospital.*

From my pocket I take the stone I keep there. I've had it a little over a year now, when Baba brought it home from the marketplace on my ninth birthday. He'd met a man selling stones of all colors and from all over. The one he gave Chanda was purple and sparkled in the light, and I wondered why he brought me this stone with layers of light and dark.

"I picked this one because I know you like a story," Baba told me, even though I hadn't asked the question out loud. "This stone has been many places and taken on many forms. The stone man said it came from a volcano—"

"What's a volcano?" I asked him.

"It's a mountain that shoots fire into the sky!"

I laughed a little then. Sometimes Baba liked to tease me. But he said it was true, that after the fire-like liquid burst through the volcano, it cooled off and hardened into stone. Then it stayed there on the volcano for a long time, with the weight of more and more layers of stone pressing down on it.

I asked Baba how the stone got so smooth.

"I wondered the same thing," he said. "The man said

the stone broke away from the volcano, and rolled and rolled until it landed in a river. Then it spent many lifetimes tumbling around in the water and all its sharp edges were smoothed away."

"This stone has been through a lot," I said.

"Yes, but it is stronger for it. A weaker stone would have crumbled away into nothing."

When I hold on to the stone now I feel a little stronger, as if Baba is still with me.

I don't remember falling asleep, but when I wake up, the sky outside the window is the blue-gray of early morning. The stone from Baba still rests in my hand. A quick glance around the hut lets me know I'm alone.

At breakfast in the courtyard my neighbors are all talking around me, but I don't hear what anyone is saying. I don't taste what I'm eating.

I spend the rest of the morning inside my house, but I can't stay away from the window. The rickshaw will come back soon, I know it will. I go outside and try to distract myself by throwing the ball with Raj, but I keep stopping to look in the direction of the city.

When Amma and Chanda still aren't back after lunchtime, I decide to fix the hole in our roof. Last week the rain leaked through our ceiling, so I set out some river grasses to dry. I've never repaired the roof by myself before, but I helped Baba sometimes.

We keep a ladder next to the cowshed, and when I

pick it up I almost fall over from the weight of it. I set it on the ground to drag it by the top rung to my house. A neighbor would help me carry it if I asked, but I want to do this myself.

I gather the grasses and twist the ends to hold them together. With the bundle of river grass tucked under my arm, I climb the rickety ladder to the roof. Raj lies down next to the ladder to wait for me.

The thatch crunches beneath my hands and knees as I crawl to the spot that leaks. I take a piece of twine from my pocket and hold it in my teeth as I work to cover the hole.

When I was a little boy, the age Chanda is now, I thought our home grew right out of the ground and that our roof was made of a tree whose branches drooped down to cover the walls. I cried when I found out I was wrong.

"I built our home from the earth, Hastin," Baba told me. "And it is made from the river, too. I mixed the river water with the dirt, until it was thick enough to make strong walls."

I asked him then about the tree that grew to make our roof.

"Also from the river," said Baba. "I gathered the reeds and grasses that grew in the water. After the sun dried them, I tied them in bundles to make our roof. That post in the middle of the hut—that is a tree trunk. I placed it in the ground myself, to hold the roof over us."

As I tie the knot that will hold the new grass on our roof, I realize I wasn't completely wrong. A tree did help to make our home. So did the earth, and the sun, and the river. But so did Baba, and that is even better.

On my way back to the ladder, I stop when I see something moving in the distance. I watch and wait as it gets closer. Finally I can make out the shape of the rickshaw, with Amar pedaling in front and Amma sitting in the back. That's all. I wait for Chanda's head to come into view next to Amma. But she isn't there.

Maybe she's lying in Amma's lap and that's why I can't see her. That has to be it.

I scramble down the ladder and jump to the ground, skipping the last three rungs. As fast as I can I run toward the rickshaw, then skid to a stop when I'm close enough to see the empty seat next to Amma.

"Where . . . ?" The rest of my question is stuck in my throat. I point to the seat where Chanda should be.

"Let's go inside," Amma says as she climbs out of the rickshaw. All the eyes of our neighbors are on us as we walk to our hut.

Inside, we sit down next to each other and I lean against Amma. Neither of us speaks. Maybe we're both trying to hang on to this moment, when everything feels safe and all we need is each other.

She brushes my hair back with her hand. My wavy hair and round face are like Baba's. I wonder if Amma still sees him when she looks at me, and if the reminder hurts or makes her happy.

"Amma, where is Chanda?"

"I had to leave her at the hospital. The doctors think she will be all right, with the treatment they are giving her."

"But how much will that cost?"

It seems Amma is not going to answer. Finally she says, "Four thousand rupees."

"Four thousand rupees! That's—"

"Yes, four thousand rupees is more than we have. If I sewed day and night and we stopped eating until the year's end, it's still more than we'd have."

"So what now? How will she get better if we'll never have so much money?"

"Amar knew of a man who could loan us the money. The man—his name is Raju Sharma—sent a worker with the money for Chanda's care. The whole four thousand! He handed it over like he was buying a bag of flour. Can you imagine it?" She looks like she is staring at something far away.

"We cannot lose her, Hastin. There is no way I could ever pay what the doctors wanted. Then there was this person who could take care of everything, and I told them yes, please help us. What else could I do?"

"How will we pay him back?"

Before she turns away, I see how tired she looks.

"I'll work in the factory," I offer.

"No!" Amma looks into my eyes.

Others have done this, like my best friend, Ajay. Many of the carpet factory workers are younger than I am.

"But you already work so hard," I say. "And Chanda will need you at home to take care of her when she's well. Let me help."

"You've seen the children who come back from those places."

She is right. When Ajay returned after a year of work, he looked like an old person, hunched over and too thin. He couldn't stop coughing from the dust that filled the factory day after day. Thinking about it makes my throat scratchy.

I hang my head. "Then how do we pay back Sharmaji?"

"He needs a new maid to clean his house in the city."

"In the city? So we have to move there?" I glance around our hut and out the window toward the courtyard. Everything I know is here.

"No, Hastin, just me."

So I will be alone? I hold my breath, as if caught in a sandstorm with no cloth to cover my face.

"I need you to stay here to take care of our home. When Chanda is well enough, Amar will drive you to the hospital to pick her up. I will talk to the neighbors before I leave. I'm sure they'll help you." She takes both of my hands in hers. "I'm sorry—I have to do this for Chanda. It would be different if your father were still here. But he is gone and so are his carvings. I wish I knew another way."

"It's all right, Amma." I wipe the tears from her face and try my best to look brave. But I worry I'll never feel safe again.

Chanda will get better, and Amma found a way to take care of us and pay the hospital. It strikes me then that my prayers have been answered.

3

Family members will encourage an injured elephant to stand and rejoin the herd.

—From Care of Jungle Elephants *by Tin San Bo*

After Amma has been gone for a week, Amar offers to take me to visit her. "My brother wants to sell his camel, but he's too old to make the trip to the market himself," he tells me. "Take care of the camel this week, then ride with me to the city and we'll surprise your mother."

I'm happy to have the work. It keeps my mind off my loneliness. Raj has been following me around more than ever, like he knows we have only each other. He even sleeps in the house with me now. I think Amma would say it's all right.

Each morning at sunrise I cross the courtyard to

Amar's hut. After I untie the camel from her post, I lead her around while she grazes on the plants. At night I join my neighbors for dinner, then return to Amar's home to clean up after the camel and give her an evening walk. At first I tried to pet her, but now I stand as far away from her as I can. She's surprised me too many times by biting me or licking my face. I've learned to jump out of the way, but I still cannot avoid her spitting.

When I ask Amar the camel's name, he tells me she doesn't have one.

"I'll call her Moti," I say.

"You like the name Moti?" he asks.

"No. I have a cousin named Moti. He's mean and he smells bad."

"Good name," Amar says.

Moti licks my cheek. I storm off to wash my face.

At the week's end I can hardly sleep, thinking about what I'll say to Amma when I see her.

We leave before sunrise. Amar wants to make sure he has plenty of time during the shopping day to sell Moti.

I help load food and jars of water into a basket on Moti's back, then we begin our journey to the market. Raj stands in the road barking as we leave, but he doesn't follow. He hasn't liked Moti ever since she stepped on him when he got too close.

Amar and I take turns riding Moti and pedaling the rickshaw. Between the bouncing ride on the camel and the pedaling, everything on my body aches by the time we reach the city.

When we find our way to Raju Sharma's house, I stand at the end of a long driveway and look up. I wonder what it's made of. The walls are whiter than any sand I've ever seen. Many people must have worked for a long time to build this house that seems bigger than my whole village.

"This is all one house?" I ask.

"Yes, Sharmaji is a rich man."

"He must have a big family." I start to walk up the driveway.

Amar grabs my shoulder. "Come, I'll take you to the back door."

We circle the house, Amar walking with the rickshaw while I lead Moti. The yard we enter has shrubs with tops so even and flat they could be used as tables. Some of the bushes have been cut to look like huge birds. A square pool of water, larger than four huts from my village, fills the center of the yard. I step closer. The water is deep, but I can see right through it to the bottom.

"I didn't know water could be that clear."

Then I see Amma.

She stands under a papaya tree. One arm encircles a basket, and her other hand clutches a papaya she's picked off a branch. I've lived without her for two weeks, but it seems longer now. I want to grab her hand and run back home with her, where she belongs.

"Hastin?" she says. I hand Moti's rope to Amar and

run toward my mother, then stop. It looks like she's trying to make herself smile. This isn't the whole-face smile she always gets when she sees me. All this time, I thought she must be missing me as much as I've missed her, but now I'm wondering if I've done something wrong.

She glances up at the house, then drops the papaya into the basket and sets it down. Amar waits behind with Moti while I hurry across the yard to hug Amma. My stomach knots with worry when I notice blue-black skin around her left eye. In the short time since I've seen her, she looks smaller somehow, so I'm careful not to squeeze her too hard.

"I've missed you so much!" She steps back to look at me and combs my hair with her hand.

"I missed you, too, Amma."

"But why—you came all this way—is everything all right?" She looks from me to Amar.

"Yes, everything is fine. I just wanted to see you." I tell her about helping Amar with Moti. "But I don't think anyone will buy her," I say. "She bites." I show her my arm. Amma laughs and kisses the bite marks Moti has given me.

"Amma, what happened to your eye?" When I reach out, she straightens and backs up a step before I can touch her face.

She raises her hand to the bruise. "Oh, that, it's nothing," she says. "Silly me, I walked into a door!"

Something isn't right. Amma is talking much faster

than she usually does, as if to keep me from figuring out what's wrong. I feel the kind of worry I get when I first notice the change in the air that warns of a coming storm. My hand reaches into my pocket to hold Baba's stone.

She points to the house. "It is beautiful, isn't it?"

An earsplitting voice interrupts our conversation.

"Get that beast out of our yard!" Two children, a girl about my age and an older boy, stand near the back door of the house. I look to see what the girl is yelling about. Moti is nibbling on the head of one of the bird-shaped bushes as Amar tries to pull her away. I hurry toward them, then stop when a large stone flies across my path and hits the camel on the side of her head. The children laugh, then run into the house after the boy brushes dirt off of his hands.

I rush to Amar's side. "Is she all right?" I ask. My mother follows close behind me. As much as I dislike Moti, I don't want her to get hurt. How is she to know not to eat animal-shaped plants?

Amar struggles with the rope while Moti tries to break free. With one hand I grab the rope to help Amar, and with the other I pet Moti under the neck. The roughness of the rope sliding through my clutched fist burns my hand. Moti calms down and stops fighting. Before I can jump out of the way, she licks my face.

"Why does she have to do that?" I wipe off the camel slobber with my shirt.

"I should take her to the marketplace now," Amar says to my mother.

"Yes, please do." She looks toward the house, then back to Amar.

"I can stay with Hastin for a short time, then he can drive the rickshaw to the market and meet you there," Amma says. "Thank you so much for bringing him with you. I'll have more time to talk to Hastin if you come back tonight."

My legs are so worn out from our trip I feel like they'll fall off if I try to pedal again, but I do not argue. Amar tells me how to find the marketplace, then leads Moti away.

I look from one end of the house to the other. Gold and red curtains hang behind glass windows. I start to count them but lose my place.

"Which room is yours?" I ask.

"Oh, I don't live in the big house, I just work there." With a glance over her shoulder, Amma takes my hand and leads me farther into the yard. "I have to get back to work soon, but I'll show you where I live."

"How is Chanda?" I ask as we walk. "Can I see her? Will she come home soon?"

We take only a few steps before Amma answers, but the silence stretches out long enough to scare me.

"Not yet," she says. "She's not well enough to have visitors or leave the hospital."

"But is she getting better?"

We stop in front of a small shack. Amma sighs and squeezes my hand. "The doctors are hopeful."

The peeling paint that clings to the walls shows that the shack must have been white a long time ago. Amma turns the knob and pushes her shoulder against the door to open it. Insects scatter when the sunlight hits the floor.

"This is smaller than our hut," I say when we step inside.

"Yes, but it's only me. This is big enough for one person."

"How many people live in that big house? Don't they have room for you there?"

"Yes, of course they have room—there is only Sharmaji and his wife and their two children. But servants don't live in the house with the family. It's fine, really."

A blanket on the dirt floor is her bed. One of her saris soaks in a bucket of water.

This is all wrong. I thought Amma would be okay here, that this place would be nicer than our home. I was worried about how Chanda and I would get along without her. I didn't think about how she would get along without us.

"It's so hot in here," I say. Our own home has open windows to let the desert wind blow through. Here, the one window is covered with murky glass. "Can you open the window?"

"No, it's stuck. It's not so bad, though." She starts to

speak again, then drops to the ground and covers her face. I sit across from her and take her hands into mine.

"I'm going to get you out of here," I say.

Her fingertips brush the side of my face, a soft touch with a rough hand. "I have to pay back Sharmaji."

"I'll find a way to help pay him back so you can come home sooner. I don't want you working for these people."

Amma looks away and stares at the ground. A shrill voice pierces the silence.

"Where is that servant girl? What happened to my swan?"

"Does everyone in this family talk that way?" I ask.

Amma jumps up and smooths out her sari. "Sharmaji's wife. I must go. You'll come by again tonight before you go back to the village?"

"Of course." I stand up. "But I mean it, Amma. I'll find a way to get you back home."

She kisses my forehead. "Don't be silly, Hastin. I will see you tonight." She rushes out the door and grabs the papaya basket on her way to the house.

I stand on tiptoe to peek through the window. When Amma reaches the door, Raju's wife grabs her arm and yanks her into the house.

Amma cannot live like this. With trembling hands I close the door to Amma's shack and run toward the road that leads to the marketplace.

4

An orphaned elephant will try to find a new herd, but will sometimes be rejected.

—From *Care of Jungle Elephants* by Tin San Bo

Walking hurts less than pedaling now, so I leave the rickshaw at Raju Sharma's house to pick up later. It would have been wise to take a water jar from Moti's back before Amar left, but I don't think of this until I walk a few blocks in the dry heat.

When I finally turn the corner to the marketplace, I stop and look up and down the road. Shop after shop lines each side of the street as far as I can see. Some vendors have stores, and others sell their items outside from tables or booths or blankets on the ground. Baba let me come here with him once, and we found a spot on the road to sit and sell his carvings. The market seems so much bigger as I stand here alone. Finding Amar in this crowd will be harder than I thought. But certainly I will find a job here.

Some of the men who are shopping wear wrapped turbans, while some wear head coverings that hang long and straight. Other people wear clothes like I've never seen and have skin so pale they look like ghosts in the crowds of shoppers. Gray-white cattle roam the side streets or rest in the shade.

Cloth and saris of colors I have never imagined hang on lines and fill the shelves of an outdoor shop. Amma's clothes would look faded and rough next to these. Maybe I can get a job folding material and helping customers. I reach out to touch the silky fabric of a sari, then flinch and step back when the woman who runs the shop yells and smacks my hand.

The next place has tables full of metal bowls that hold spices like cinnamon and turmeric. A woman uses a mortar and pestle to grind spices in a small bowl. The heat of chili powder fills my nose.

Rows of brightly painted carvings at a wood-carver's booth catch my eye. Large and small carvings of Ganesh and other gods, and animals—elephants, tigers, and camels—sit in rows on a table. The largest carvings stand face-to-face with me, while the smallest are the size of my thumb. I pick up a tiny carved elephant, painted yellow. Its wood is smooth, but I rub a spot that should have been sanded more. And perhaps the trunk needs more detail . . .

I almost drop it when I notice the old wood-carver behind the table looking at me. For a moment I worry I spoke out loud, but the man smiles and hands me a wooden box that fits in the palm of my hand. A row of elephants marches around the sides of the box, and one large elephant covers the lid.

"Open it," says the wood-carver. "See what's inside."

I lift the lid and peek into the box. It's filled with wooden elephants, each about the size of my smallest fingernail. I cannot imagine how long it must have taken to carve each one. Holding the box close to the table, I pour them out, then line them up in a long row, trunk to tail. When I feel a gust of wind I cup my hands around the elephants to protect them.

The elephant box would be a good gift for Chanda. I imagine seeing her smile when I hand it to her.

I scoop up the elephants to put them back. Not being able to afford a gift for Chanda makes me feel as small as the elephants in my hand. Each one drops into the box with a quiet *plink*.

"You are a fine wood-carver." I hand the box back to the man. *But not as good as Baba.* "My father was a wood-carver, too."

The man smiles but says nothing while he arranges carvings on the table.

"I used to help him," I add. "He was teaching me. He said I was a fast learner." I wander to the next table. The colors are pretty and the figures well painted, but

I like the natural wood of the carvings Baba made. The elephants he carved were so lifelike, I could imagine them trumpeting and stamping through the jungle.

"Maybe you could use a helper." I pretend to take interest in a bright orange carving of a tiger and hold my breath while I wait for a response.

"My sons work for me. I have all the help I need. They are almost as good as I am."

Before he can see my disappointment, I step back and melt into the crowd of shoppers.

As I wind my way through the mob, I see jewelry stores full of gold and silver bracelets and shops where women and girls my own age sit on the ground and weave baskets.

At each place I try to convince the shop owner what a wonderful puppet maker, floor sweeper, or goat milker I would be.

"No, go away. I don't need a helper."

"Our whole family works here in our shop."

"I wouldn't be able to pay you."

Many vendors wave me away and say nothing.

The sky turns pink and orange as the sun begins to drop. Everyone will leave here before dark. I want to grab the setting sun and push it higher into the sky so I will have more time.

I rush from shop to shop now, the colors and smells and sounds of the marketplace all blending together. I don't even know what jobs I'm asking for anymore, since I've stopped looking at the items on the tables. I look only into the faces of the vendors, hoping this will be the one who will help me make everything all right again. I want them to see my face, too, to see how important this is, how desperate I am to work. But no one looks at my face.

At the end of the marketplace, I stop to catch my breath. The scent of mustard oil pulls me toward a samosa shop. The woman at the counter drops a potato mixture onto pieces of dough, then folds them into triangular packages. When she makes enough to fill a tray, she hands it to her husband. With a slotted spoon, the man lowers the samosas into a black pot, heated by a flame that burns underneath. My mouth waters as the samosas tumble and bump into one another in the sea of bubbling oil. When they are fried golden brown, he removes them with the spoon and places them into paper-lined baskets.

"You like samosas?" the woman asks me.

"Yes, I do."

"Ten rupees."

My hands search my pockets as if some long-forgotten coin will suddenly appear. I start to mention what a good cook I am but can't bear the thought of being turned down again. Then I think of my mother—her black eye, the shack, the screaming family.

"I can help you sell your samosas," I say to the woman as she folds the dough. "I'll take baskets of them around the marketplace, then bring the money back to you."

The woman laughs. "I cannot send our food into the marketplace with a boy I don't know."

"Then I can help you make more," I suggest. "It looks like you are very busy. You don't have to pay me at first. You'll see what a good worker I am before you hire me."

"Don't you see this small space we have here?" she snaps. "We are bumping into each other as it is." She turns back to her work.

With nowhere else to go, I sit on the ground nearby and rest against the wall. I look back at the shops that make up the marketplace. The vendors are packing up their things for the day. Some carry boxes up a flight of stairs to their homes above their shops.

I turn toward the sound of clinking glasses. A boy who looks a little younger than I am strides by. The wire basket he carries has eight spaces for holding tea glasses. He seems to be in a hurry, yet hardly anything spills from the two glasses that are still full. The man and woman at the samosa booth greet him with a smile. He hands them each a glass of tea. My eyes follow the coins that pass from the samosa vendor's hand to the boy's, then to his pocket. The man hands him two more coins, which the boy puts into his other pocket. He chats with them as they drink their tea, then they hand him the empty glasses.

He hurries away with his tea rack and turns down a nearby side street. I jump up to follow him.

5

An elephant can be coaxed with words better than with physical force.

—From Care of Jungle Elephants *by Tin San Bo*

Down the streets of the marketplace I follow the tea boy. I pass a group of children and watch them break a piece of roti into small pieces to share. When I look up, I've lost sight of the boy. I hurry down the street and stop to catch my breath when I reach the corner. To my right, nothing but cows and a few shoppers and vendors leaving for home. I scan the thinning crowd, then run down the road to my left—and smack into the back of the tea boy.

He curses as he topples forward. I stand frozen in place and watch him fall. With both hands he clutches his rack of empty glasses and holds it out in front of him. The glasses clink and rattle against the metal rack. Clouds of dust puff up when he lands with a thud and an *ooof*, stomach-first onto the ground. Both of us look at the tea rack, and I sigh with relief when I see the undamaged glasses.

I reach out my hand. "Sorry!"

The boy ignores me and gently sets the rack down before pushing himself up.

I stare at the ground. "I wasn't looking and . . ."

"Well, you should watch where you're going! If these glasses broke I'd owe more money than I earned today," he says.

"Are you all right?" I ask.

He inspects each glass more closely. "Yes, nothing is broken—on me or the glasses."

"I'm Hastin."

He nods. "I'm Yusuf." He brushes the dirt off his clothes.

"I've been looking for a job all day. Everyone turned me down. I saw you selling tea and thought you could tell me where to get a job like that."

"I don't know anyone who needs a tea boy."

"I have to find something—anything!" As we walk down the road, I tell Yusuf about everything that brought me to the marketplace—Chanda's illness, Amar and Moti, my mother's job with Sharma's family.

"Even if someone did hire you today," says Yusuf, "to earn four thousand rupees you would have to work for . . ." He starts to count on his fingers. ". . . a very long time."

We pass a few shops that remain open. The scent of spices fills the air at a booth where jars of pickled mangoes line the shelves. A woman chops mangoes and limes and tosses them into a vat of mustard oil. She adds a small piece of wood to the fire below a pan of roasting spices. Smoke billows toward her, and she covers her face with the end of her sari, reminding me of Amma.

"I don't care how long it takes," I say.

"There was a man at the café talking to Naresh—that's my boss. He's looking for a boy to take care of an elephant for his circus."

"An elephant? Around here?" I ask.

"No, not here—too hot and dry. Do you like animals?"

"Yes—except for camels."

"The job sounds fun!" says Yusuf. "Living in the jungle, and Timir—that's the circus man's name—Timir said that people from all over the world will come see the elephant do tricks. If he's still at the café, you can ask him about the job. I have to return the tea glasses to Naresh and give him his money."

"Give him his money?" I ask. "But you're the one selling the tea—why do you have to pay him?"

"I get to keep some, but Naresh is the one who buys the tea and makes it, so he keeps most of the money. And whenever I break a glass—I still hate to think how much I'd owe him if these broke when you ran into me!"

I stop walking and back up a few steps to look down the road we just passed.

"Wait, there's Moti!"

"You mean that camel? I thought you hated her," Yusuf says as he follows me down the side street.

"Yes, but maybe that's Amar on the other side of her."

As we approach I see that it is Amar, arguing with a customer about Moti's price. I raise an arm to stop Yusuf from walking too close to Moti. We wait and listen.

"Twenty thousand rupees is a fair price for such a fine animal!" says Amar.

"But it will cost money to feed her! I let my cow go free because her food cost me forty-five rupees a day."

"Yes, but that was a cow," says Amar. "A camel is not so picky. Give her some straw, or let her graze on the cactus around your home. Much cheaper. Take her home for only seventeen thousand rupees."

"I don't know . . ." The man turns to leave.

Amar touches his arm. "Did I mention their milk? Much better quality than cow's milk. Some say it has healing powers! Use what you need for your family and have plenty left to sell. More money for you. Only sixteen thousand rupees."

"He's good," Yusuf whispers.

"I can pay thirteen thousand," says the customer.

35

We laugh when Amar clutches his heart in horror. "Thirteen thousand!" He shakes his head. "I could never let her go for such a low price. What other animal can carry you across the desert without stopping for a drink?" He waves his hands at some imaginary desert in front of him. "Fifteen thousand. That's as low as I can go."

The man sighs. Amar leans forward, waiting for his answer. Yusuf and I lean forward, too. Even Moti stares at the man, as if she, too, is anxious to hear his decision. Just when I think the man will walk away, he reaches into his pocket.

"All right, fifteen thousand," he says as he pulls out a stack of bills. The two men shake hands, then Moti's new owner takes her rope and leads her away.

"There you are," says Amar when he notices me.

"This is Yusuf," I say. "He's showing me the café where he works. Can I meet you back at Raju Sharma's house? I left the rickshaw there."

"I suppose that's all right," says Amar. "But don't take too long."

We finally arrive at Naresh's café. A laughing figure of Ganesh sits in the window, holding a tea glass. A ringing cowbell announces our arrival when Yusuf pushes open the door.

The few customers in the café sit at round wooden tables while they talk, eat, and drink tea. One man wipes off a countertop with an old rag while he talks with a man at the table near him. My stomach reminds me how hungry I am when it growls at the smell of spices and bread and brewing tea.

Yusuf motions for me to follow as he approaches the man behind the counter. He sets the tea rack down and removes the money from his left-hand pocket. He hands it to the man, who must be Naresh. Yusuf does not touch his right-hand pocket, which holds the extra coins the samosa vendor gave him. Naresh puts most of the money away in the cash register, then hands a few coins back to Yusuf.

"Who's your friend?" he asks.

Yusuf introduces me to Naresh and Timir, the man who sits at the table. I feel like I'm staring at a skull—his face is thin and pale, as if he hasn't seen the sun for a long time. He seems older than my mother. Some gray streaks his long hair and black beard. But his hand that rests on the ivory handle of his cane looks soft and smooth, like the skin of a new calf. The sunlight through the window catches the red stone in his thick gold ring.

"Hastin is looking for a job," says Yusuf.

"Yes, I need to work so my mother can go home," I say. "She works for a man named Raju Sharma."

"And how does a boy like you plan to get your mother away from Raju Sharma?" Timir asks.

I force my eyes away from his steaming cup of tea on the table. My mouth would be watering if it were not so dry. "She is working for him because my sister is sick, and he paid for her treatment. If I get a job, I can help pay him back and my mother can go home sooner." My stomach growls out loud.

Timir smiles. "Naresh, bring a cup of tea for each of the boys. And a basket of samosas." He points to the chairs across from him, inviting us to sit down.

"So, about your sister," says Timir. "What happens if she's well enough to go home, and you and your mother are both working?"

I can't believe I didn't think of this. If I find a job, both Amma and I will be away from home until we earn enough money to pay back Sharma.

"My neighbors in our village will take care of her." I try to answer as if I'm sure of myself and have everything planned, but it ends up sounding more like a question.

"I need to hire a boy," says Timir. "Years ago I ran a circus, and I plan to bring it back, starting with the elephant show. I'm looking for someone to care for the elephant. But it is hard work. Do you have experience working with animals?"

"He's an expert in camel care," says Yusuf.

"How much does your mother owe Sharmaji?" Timir asks.

"Four thousand rupees," I answer.

"That is a lot of money." Timir takes a sip of his tea.

"I just saw a man pay fifteen thousand for a camel."

He laughs. "A fair price. If I were talking to a camel

right now I might offer him fifteen thousand rupees myself."

I look down at the table.

"But it will pay better than any job you can get around here. And more of an adventure!" Timir leans forward. "Think of it—living in the jungle! No more desert sand blowing in your eyes." He pauses while Naresh places cups of hot tea and a basket of steaming samosas in front of us.

"Don't forget the people from all over the world," Yusuf says.

"That's right!" says Timir. "From all over the world, they will come see the elephant stand on its head, walk through hoops, give rides—lots of tricks. And you will have the most important job—taking care of the star of the show!"

I smile at Yusuf, then at Timir. "What's the elephant's name?" I bite into the edge of a samosa, using only my teeth, so the hot filling will not burn my tongue.

Timir looks over his shoulder before answering. "We have to catch one. That will be your first job when you get to the circus grounds."

"I have to catch an elephant?"

"*Chup!* You fool!" He hushes me. He leans in so close I can't escape his piercing glare. "Keep your voice down about this."

He leans back but keeps his voice in a low whisper.

"I've hired workmen to dig a trap in the jungle. Every day you'll check it and let me know when we've caught an elephant."

I don't like the idea of capturing an elephant from the jungle, but I know I cannot work as an elephant caretaker without an elephant.

"I am a hard worker," I say. "But—how much does the job pay?"

Timir leans back and stares up at the ceiling of the café. "Like I said, it will be hard work, and you will be away from home for a long time. I think five thousand rupees is fair."

When I feel my eyes widen I look away and hope Timir does not notice my disbelief. I stare at a spot on the wall while I pretend to consider the offer. Out of the corner of my eye I notice Timir's grin. Yusuf leans toward me and kicks me under the table.

Timir adds, "Of course, I will provide all your food and living quarters."

I nod. "Five thousand rupees. Yes, I suppose that would be enough. I'll do it." I take a drink of my tea.

"You're sure a year isn't too long to be away from your family?" Timir says.

My sip of tea feels stuck in my throat. I hadn't thought to ask how long I'd have to work to earn my pay.

"A year?" My hand reaches for the stone in my pocket.

"Yes, I am paying a lot of money for your service. It's

worth more than a year of your time. But if you're not sure . . ."

"No, it's fine. And I'm sure I'll come home to visit now and then."

"The circus is too far away. You'll be too busy to leave anyway. But you're right, I should not ask a young boy to leave home for so long. I've seen plenty of older boys around who could use a job." He stands and grabs his cane.

"No, please!" My chair falls over when I jump up. "You don't need to ask anyone else. I'll do the job—I want to do it."

"This is a big responsibility," Timir says. "If I hire you, I have to know I can depend on you, and that you're not going to make any trouble about wanting to go home."

"No, I won't be any trouble. I can do the job. I just worry about my mother missing me too much."

Timir leans over so he is eye to eye with me, and the hair on the back of my neck stands up. "Honestly, your mother would never say this to you, but think about how else this will help her. One less mouth to feed." He straightens up and holds out his hand. "So we have a deal?"

I shake Timir's hand. His long fingers curl around my hand, crushing it in his grip, and his ring digs into my palm.

"So what do we do about Sharmaji?" I ask when Timir lets go.

"I will take care of that. You go home and pack. I'll bring your mother home to you tomorrow morning and pick you up then."

I thank Yusuf and say goodbye to him and Naresh before leaving the café.

As tired as I am, I start running down the street toward Raju Sharma's house to tell Amma the good news. She is going home! I'm able to help my family after all, and already I feel more grown up.

Early the next morning at my village, I sit inside Timir's truck as he talks to my mother. "Don't worry, Parvati," he says. "I'll take good care of your boy. He will be quite happy, I promise."

"Give me one more minute, please," Amma says, wiping tears from her face.

We have said goodbye many times, but she approaches the open window of the truck once again. She takes my hands and places something in my palm.

I feel the smooth wood of my father's pocketknife. The knife he used for his carvings. "Amma, are you sure?"

"Baba wanted you to have it. I was saving it for when you were older, but . . ."

"Thank you. I'll be careful with it."

Amma nods. "Now, be brave, and be a good worker. Do what Timir says." She lets go of my hands and steps away from the truck. "I will see you next year."

The truck rolls past my home, Raj running alongside and barking. I turn to the back window to watch Amma, still standing in the road. As we drive farther away she grows smaller and smaller, her face just a dot of cinnamon and the green of her sari blowing in the wind.

6

Between the ages of six and fifteen, male elephants must begin caring for themselves, away from the herd.
—From *Care of Jungle Elephants* by Tin San Bo

The cloth rice bag on my lap holds all that I own, except for the stone from Baba. I take it from my pocket now. I shield my eyes from the sunlight as we start the long ride to my new workplace.

During most of the drive, Timir brags about the circus he used to run. "The elephant show is the first step in bringing the circus back to life. My circus was the best around, before it was closed," he says. "We had the greatest animal acts—bears riding cycles, and a dancing bear who wore a dress. We had trained tigers and lions, and so many clowns—"

"Clowns?" I ask.

"Yes, men who paint their faces with makeup and do tricks—"

"Makeup?"

"Yes, makeup. You know, like women wear, but clowns wear a lot more."

I shake my head.

"Maybe you've seen women on television wearing makeup."

I've never seen television. "No," I say. "Did the clowns wear dresses, too, like the bears?"

"No, you're missing the point!" He slaps the steering wheel. "The clowns dressed funny and did tricks that made the audience laugh. And the monkeys—they have arms and legs like people, but are much smaller—"

"I know what a monkey is." Now my new boss must think I'm stupid, so I do not ask him if the monkeys wore clothes, too. I stare out the window and listen quietly while he chatters away about his trapeze artists, acrobats, and tightrope walkers.

I don't ask what those things are, and I don't ask what I am wondering most of all. If Timir's circus was so great, why did it close down?

We leave the sands of the desert behind us. Brown has turned to green during our drive, at first with a lonely tree here and there, then clumps of them standing closer and closer. Now they're so thick there's nothing but trees on either side of us.

Timir pulls off the treelined road, then parks the truck next to a barbed-wire fence that surrounds a large clearing.

"Here we are." He opens the door and steps out of the truck. I climb out, too, clutching my rice bag, and follow Timir through a large wooden gate. He leads me to a fence made of rotten wood, tangled with vines, that encircles an area filled with tall brown grass. So many posts are missing, the fence reminds me of an old person's teeth. The trees are thick behind the fence, so I can't see what's beyond.

Timir beams at the rotten wooden benches, vine-wrapped fence, and frayed ropes hanging from high wooden poles like he's a father showing off a new son. There must be some mistake. This cannot be what Timir has been bragging about during our whole trip.

"So—this is your circus?" I ask.

"It was." He turns to me. "And it will be again. The elephant act is the start. As we make money from that, we will add other acts, until we have the full circus running." He steps onto a bench, then stumbles when it falls apart beneath him. He glares at the bench, as if he is angry at it for crumbling. "You'll need to build new benches before our first show." He points to the fence. "And fix the arena fence. Follow me."

Timir leads me away from the arena and through the trees to a building that looks like the shack Amma lived in behind Raju's house. It's bigger, but made of wood, and it has a flat roof and peeling white paint. Inside is a desk piled with stacks of papers and a brown sofa against one wall.

"My office," says Timir. "You're never to enter without permission. I'll call you when it needs cleaning, or if you're in trouble." He smiles down at me and puts a hand on my shoulder. "But you don't plan on causing any trouble, do you?"

I feel like backing away from that smile, but his grip on my shoulder is so strong I can't move. My throat tightens up, so I shake my head to answer Timir's question.

"Good. A smart boy."

I rub my tingling shoulder as soon as Timir releases it and turns away.

"Come, I'll show you the cook shed."

We stop in front of a large building that's open on one side, so it has only three walls. The high thatched roof and walls made of mud remind me of home. I wonder if I can sleep here.

An old man in the cook shed is kneading roti dough on a countertop lined with spice jars. Next to him is a clay stove, its chimney sticking out through the roof to let the smoke outside. On the other side of the room is a long wooden table with a bench on either side.

Timir points to the man. "You will help our cook prepare meals each day and clean the cook shed."

I can't imagine when I will have time to take care of an elephant with all the cleaning, cooking, fence repair, and building of benches.

The man looks up from the counter.

"Ne Min," he says. He nods his head once and smiles at me.

"I'm Hastin."

Ne Min isn't much taller than I am, and his hair is thin and white. The lines around his eyes look like they're used to being wrinkled up from smiling, but I think there's something sad about his eyes, too.

"Where are you from?" I ask, because I've never heard a name or an accent like his before.

"Burma," he says. "But that was a long time ago." He turns back to the dough. Yes, there is something sad about his eyes, and I wonder why he's so far from home.

Outside, Timir shows me a small wooden building behind the cook shed where I'll find all the tools and cleaning supplies I'll need. Beyond that is the barbed-wire fence and another wooden gate. This one is narrow and opens to a dirt path that stretches into the woods. Parked behind the fence is a mud-splattered white truck.

"This way to your sleeping quarters," Timir says. He leads me past a row of rusty metal cages to a box-shaped building, taller than any of the others. Like the arena fence, it is made of logs. A trough and a stack of hay bales sit near one wall. A metal bucket hangs by its handle on one end of the trough.

"Bet you've never seen an elephant stable before," Timir says. I shake my head, then peer inside when he pulls open the door. This is much bigger than our cowshed at home.

Four cows standing side by side could fit in here. A gray blanket lies on a thick bed of straw that covers the floor.

Timir points to a nail, high on one wall. "Hang your bag there."

"You mean—I'll sleep here?" I ask.

"Of course. The elephant keeper must live with the elephant. When it gets hungry at night, or cold, you'll need to be nearby to take care of it."

When I step to the wall to hang up my rice bag, a small field mouse scurries across the straw. Its fur is the color of sand, the color of home. I want to pick up the mouse and tell it that it doesn't have to leave just because I'll be living here. Maybe it will stay if I bring it a bite of my dinner each night.

I peek through the gaps between the logs of the stable walls and don't see any other buildings. "Where does everyone else sleep?" I ask Timir.

"The rest of us return to our homes nearby every night. Don't worry, you won't be sleeping alone for long. My workmen are in the woods now, digging a trap for our new elephant. Every evening before dinner you will leave through the gate I parked next to and follow the path to the trap. Once you check it, you will report back to me. At no other time are you to leave the grounds. Once the elephant is caught, there won't be any reason for you to leave at all." He points at the woods behind him with his cane. "Through there you'll find the spring on the property where you'll bathe the elephant."

He glances at the mouse, now sniffing the wood of the stable door. With one smooth motion Timir raises his cane and swings it toward the ground. The tip of the cane smacks the mouse with a *crack*. I jump back and hit the stable wall. My stomach sinks as I stare at the broken animal on the ground. I blink to hold back the tears that burn my eyes.

Timir tosses up the cane, grabs its handle, and continues his instructions as if nothing happened. "The elephant trainer, Sharad, will show you the trap."

I worry that if I ever get in Timir's way, he will crush me as easily as he did the mouse.

7

Since she is most aware of danger, the oldest female
leads the herd.

            —From *Care of Jungle Elephants* by Tin San Bo

Sharad reminds me of a round toad walking on its hind legs, as wide as he is tall. Even his eyes are a bit like a toad's, like he's always surprised. When he talks to me, I try to look at his face, but my eyes drift to his head. I think he is mostly bald, but the hair he does have grows long. He combs it into a swirled pile that rests on his head like a coiled snake ready to strike.

He leads me through the forest to a banyan tree that stands next to a river. "Come here late in the afternoon to see if we've caught anything," he tells me. We're standing at the edge of the trap beneath the tree. I wonder how long it took the workmen to dig a hole this size. The trap is wide enough for a man to lie down in. Sharad moves aside some of the branches that hide its opening. I peer into the darkness of the pit and take a step back. If I fell in there I wouldn't be able to climb out on my own.

"Won't the elephant get hurt in the fall?" I ask.

He points into the trap. "That's what the leaves are for." I lean in a little closer. A blanket of leaves covers the bottom of the pit. "Enough there to work as a cushion."

He rearranges the branches to hide the trap again. "If the herd is around when you arrive, stay out of their way. Watch them from a tree. After a day or two, we will have our elephant."

When Sharad brought me to the trap, we rode in his truck, which took only a few minutes. That first day I discover it takes much longer on foot. I am used to walking on flat ground, not these hills, so by the time I reach the trap I have to stop to catch my breath and rest my burning leg muscles.

The forest also holds many things that bite. There are more mosquitoes here than at home—I swat my way through buzzing gray clouds and try to ignore my worries that their bites could make me sick. Red bites dot my hands, ankles, face—any skin my clothing doesn't protect.

One branch of the banyan tree, ripe with figs, hangs low over the pit. The large elephants have to walk around it, but it's high enough for a young elephant to walk under—then into the trap. Just what Timir wants.

I grab on to a limb to climb the tree, then leap back when something crawls across my fingers. I shake out my hand and rub it on my shirt. Before touching the tree again I check all the branches for whatever animals might be living in them.

The tree looks clear, so I climb up and find a branch to sit on while I wait for the elephants. With my pocket-knife I cut a thin branch to whittle. My knife slices away curls of bark that float down to the trap.

When the stick is peeled away to nothing I put my knife back in my pocket and look out at the treetops. Never have I seen this much green. One tree blends into another, and another, so I cannot tell where one tree ends and the next begins. Green surrounds me with its leafy walls, covers the ground below me, and hangs over my head in a canopy of branches. It is beautiful but it is not my home, with its browns of rust-tan mud and sand and thatch.

I hear the elephants before I see them. The snapping of twigs and rustle of leaves catch my attention. Then I see the waves of gray weaving through the trees in front of me.

Some elephants run ahead of the herd, calling out trumpet blasts as they plunge into the water. Others stay close to the riverbank, rolling in the mud or ripping branches from a mango tree. They're so close I can hear them chewing leaves and fruit.

The smallest ones stand right next to the adults, even

underneath them. Maybe those are their parents, but I wonder how they can tell who's who. They all look the same to me, one body of gray after another.

Two elephant calves spray each other with water, then entwine their trunks and flop into the river together. I long to jump from the tree and play in the water with them.

After the herd spends time drinking and splashing in the river and eating from the trees, the largest elephant rolls to a stand on the riverbank, coated with mud. She calls out a rumbling trumpet and walks along the path toward the banyan tree. The rest of the elephants pour one last trunkful of water into their mouths or take another splash in the river before climbing up the bank to follow her.

I clutch a branch of the tree as the herd approaches. The adult elephants walk around the branch that hangs over the trap. The babies follow them so closely, they miss the trap, too. The older calves are in the most danger. They follow the herd, but don't cling to their mothers' sides like the smallest ones do. The pair I watched playing are at the back of the herd now, walking closer to the trap. A large elephant turns and grumbles at them, and the two calves run to catch up. I laugh when they take their places at her side—the side farther from the trap. When she walks around the hanging branch, they do, too.

When the last elephant is out of sight, I jump down

from the banyan tree and start my journey back to the circus grounds.

On my way to the cook shed to help prepare dinner, I stop at the doorway of Timir's office. He looks up from the paperwork in front of him and places his hands flat on his desk as if he's going to stand up.

"Well?" he says.

I shake my head and try to look disappointed. Timir slaps his desk and sinks back into his chair. He glances up and motions me away. I smile all the way to the cook shed.

The straw on the stable floor makes a bed that's soft but scratchy. I keep moving my blanket around to try to get comfortable. Finally I pull my collar up to keep the straw from chafing my neck.

Calls of animals in the distance echo in a jumble of hoots, chirps, whirrs, and screeches. Something skitters across the roof of the stable, its nails clicking against the wood. Lying here in the dark, it strikes me how completely alone I am. Alone in a way I never knew before. When Amma took Chanda to the hospital, I was by myself in our hut, but my neighbors were nearby. Things I'd known all my life surrounded me. I had the mud walls and thatched roof that Baba made. I had Raj, and the ball of fabric scraps I threw to him. I had Ganesh.

From my pocket I take my knife and unfold the blade from the handle. I roll to my side so I'm facing the stable wall. On a log closest to me, I scratch a line with my knife. I'll use this log to count the days until I can return home.

"One," I whisper.

Amma is probably asleep now, but I can't help wondering if she is thinking of me, too. And I wonder how Chanda is doing. I wish we could all go back to the way things were, before one bite from a mosquito changed everything.

Stars peek through the spaces between the logs that make up the stable walls. I try to count them to keep my mind off home and the noises outside.

Over the next few days, I work harder than I ever have before. Sharad shows me the woodshed, close to the arena, where I'll store the wood I chop to keep it dry until we need it. Sharad and the other men are also helping to repair the arena fence with the larger pieces of wood. I carry smaller pieces to the cook shed when the stack next to the stove runs low. The other men keep working when I stop to help Ne Min prepare meals. Timir stays in his office. I don't know what he does in there all day.

Before each meal, I take the metal tub from the cook shed to the spring on the circus grounds and fill it with water. It takes a long time to carry it back because I have to keep stopping to rest my arms. My legs knock against the tub as I walk, splashing some of the water onto the ground.

In the cook shed I place the tub on the stove and light the fire. Ne Min uses some of the water for cooking, and we use the rest for washing dishes after the meal. Ne Min does not cook like my mother. Often I don't know what I'm eating, but my plate looks so clean after each meal no one would guess there had been food on it minutes earlier.

Every afternoon when I get to the trap I'm relieved to see that the leafy branches and grass that hide the opening of the trap are untouched. The first morning Ne Min gave me a cup of dry besan to take to the spring with me to help with the mosquito bites. The flour helped calm the itching when I bathed with it. He also gave me a bottle of neem-oil. I do not like its smell—a bit like rotten eggs—but Ne Min said the mosquitoes don't like it either, and he was right. The mosquitoes don't bother me now.

Today the elephants are already at the river when I arrive, so I climb a mango tree to watch them. I climb as high as I can, then find a good branch to sit on. Branches overhead sway with a new breeze, and I cover my face to protect it from the stinging sand that does not come. I still forget that no dry sand will blow here. I drop my hands and feel the breeze on my face.

Some of the elephants wade into the river, filling their trunks and spraying water over their backs. The more I watch them, the more I see I was wrong about them all looking the same. Most are dark gray, but some have skin that's lighter gray, like the sky just before sunrise. Some are gray all over, while others have splotches of pink on their faces and trunks. A few young elephants have the beginning of tusks. One elephant I recognize by her tattered ears, another by her droopy eyes.

The two calves who played in the river my first day are my favorites. One always looks like she is smiling, and the other has skin the color of moonlight through a storm cloud. I have named them Nandita and Indurekha—Joyful and Moonbeam. After wrestling and splashing in the river, they lie down and roll in the mud of the riverbank.

I wonder which elephants are the mothers of Nandita and Indurekha. It is hard to tell, since they are all protective of the calves. When the young ones wander too far and an elephant rumbles at them, I think, "So that one, Bindu, with the spotted trunk, must be a mother." But then Patala, with the pink face, is the first to rush to the babies when a tiger growls in the distance, so then I'm not sure. The other adults respond the same way when the calves are in danger, so I give up trying to figure out which ones are the mothers.

Nandita stands up, wearing a coat of mud, and stretches her trunk toward the mango branches below me. She squeaks a complaint when she finds that the fruit-filled branches are too high. Indurekha rolls up from the bank. Her trunk brushes the tip of a branch but cannot reach the mangoes either.

With a glance at the herd, I climb to a lower branch of the tree. I grasp the branch next to me and bend it toward the elephant calves. Indurekha's trunk curls around a mango, then she drops the whole fruit into her mouth. Nandita wraps her trunk around the branch and pulls, as if she is trying to rip the branch from the tree. With my other hand I keep a tight grip on the branch I'm sitting on.

When Indurekha bites into her second mango, Nandita gives up trying to take the whole branch and instead grabs one fruit. She watches me as she quickly pops it into her mouth.

The calves flap their ears and turn to the herd, which is starting to move away from the river. The largest elephant leads the way, and the other adults keep their young close as they walk.

I know I was hired to be the elephant keeper, but the more time I spend with the elephants, the less I want to trap one. I see them play together, like Chanda and I used to play. They eat together, and I think of everyone at home gathering around the courtyard stove.

From my pocket I take Baba's stone and hold it in my hand. I cling to the mango tree and hold my breath as the herd walks along the path where the trap waits. One by one, the elephants pass by the hidden pit and continue up the trail that leads away from the river. Safe for one more day.

8

In the presence of danger, all members of the herd encircle and protect a calf.
        —From *Care of Jungle Elephants* by Tin San Bo

Timir's anger grows each time I tell him that no elephant has fallen into the trap. What will happen if we never catch an elephant? It's now been a week that they have safely passed by. They must be smarter than Timir thinks they are.

I dread the sound of Timir's angry yelling when I tell him that yet again we failed to catch an elephant. But the sound I dread even more is that of an elephant crashing into the trap.

Today when I climb the banyan tree to watch the elephants, dark storm clouds swirl over the forest. I grasp a branch and hold my breath as the herd leaves the riverbank. They move closer to the trap below me and I stare at its covering of branches and leaves, praying the elephants will safely avoid it again. That's it, walk around it, I think as one by one they pass it by.

Nandita lags behind, and an older elephant nudges her with her trunk. When I lean forward for a better look, the branch I grab shakes. A ripe fig from the banyan tree falls through the air. The fruit lands on the branches that hide the trap's opening.

Nandita turns to the fig. She reaches for it, and her foot brushes the edge of the trap.

"No!" I yell. At the sound of my voice, Nandita darts forward. The cover of branches and leaves falls away when she tumbles and disappears into the pit. I hear a crash, then a howling cry.

Branches shake as the elephants bellow and run circles around the banyan tree. Some of the elephants reach their trunks into the trap to grab Nandita's trunk and pull. But the hole is too deep. I press my hands against my ears to try to block out the herd's painful wails and screams.

I don't know how much time passes, but when the herd finally grows quiet, the forest is growing dark. The largest elephant turns to continue leading the herd down the path. One by one the others follow. The leader grumbles at the few who stay behind and call to Nandita, who cries out from the trap. Soon they, too, leave the riverbank.

One last elephant remains near the trap. She is the

quiet one I call Sanjana. The tree shudders at her thundering roar of fury.

Nandita's mother.

It starts to rain, and the banyan tree shelters me with its tangle of branches. I watch and listen to the mother elephant and her baby call to each other. A few elephants from the herd stop and call to Sanjana.

She wails and paces back and forth in front of the trap. What if she never leaves? I might have to stay in this tree all night.

With one last touch of her trunk to her child, Sanjana turns away to join the herd. After every few steps, she looks back and cries out to Nandita again. Long after the elephants are out of sight, the wailing echoes through the forest.

Nandita's mother has left her. She will be without her family now, and it's all my fault.

I scramble down the tree. At the edge of the trap, I lean forward to peer into the darkness of the pit. The smell of wet earth and rotten leaves hangs thick in the air. When a movement of gray lets me know that Nandita is pacing the floor of the trap, I sigh with relief. The blanket of leaves was enough to protect her when she fell. The young elephant still cries out from the trap.

"Shhh, you'll be all right. I'll take care of you," I tell her. "I'm sorry," I add, because I am one of her captors.

Even in the dark her eyes look wild and scared. I think

back to Amma, desperate to find a way to make Chanda well. If I were strong enough, I would pull Nandita out of the trap and lead her through the forest to her family.

But I can't help her now. I'll have to go tell Timir about Nandita, but I don't want to leave without doing something for her.

I run to the mango tree and snap off the limb with the largest fruit. When I return to the trap, I lie down and lower the mango branch into the pit.

"Here—are you hungry?"

She grabs the branch and yanks it from my hand. A jagged twig scrapes my palm.

"*Aieee!* Be patient! I'm trying to help you." I shake my stinging hand. Nandita still paces around the trap, calling to the herd. I wish I could help her understand what's going on. I am away from my family, too, but at least I know why.

"Don't worry, I'll be back." I walk away from Nandita.

I stop to glance once more at what I am leaving behind in the jungle. A knot of betrayal sits in my stomach as I turn away to return to the circus grounds.

Rain has soaked through my clothes by the time I see the glow of lantern light in the cook shed. I'm so late that Ne Min must have made dinner without me. My shivering body is ready to be in front of the oven fire, but I slow as I approach.

The elephant will be all right. I will take good care of

her. She'll be happy with me. Just as I reach the shed, I remember Timir's words to my mother, before he drove me away from my village. *"Don't worry, Parvati. I'll take good care of your boy. He will be quite happy, I promise."*

Everyone is sitting at the table, eating dinner. When they notice me the room grows quiet. My hand goes to my pocket and the comfort of the stone.

I look at the ground. "Sorry. Still no elephant."

9

An elephant will not step where it does not feel safe.
— From *Care of Jungle Elephants* by Tin San Bo

Timir flings his plate across the room. I jump back when it shatters against the wall. His unfinished dinner slides to the floor. Timir's face reminds me of an overripe tomato ready to burst in the heat. He reaches across the table and grabs Sharad by the shirt. His voice carries throughout the cook shed like the hiss of a snake.

"How many elephants are there in India?"

Sharad's eyes scan the room, as if someone here has the answer. "I don't know—thousands."

"Then how is it possible you cannot manage to catch even one?" Timir releases him with a shove, and Sharad tumbles to the floor.

"Tomorrow morning, you idiots are going to dig a new trap—in a place where you can catch something this time. Enough of this waiting!"

He turns to me then. "And what took you so long?" he yells.

"The elephants—they stayed at the river longer than usual. I waited for them to walk by the trap."

He points his cane at me. "No more playing around in the woods!" he says before he storms out.

Dinnertime here is so different from home. Here there is too much heat, and too much noise. Not that mealtimes in our courtyard are quiet, but noise made of laughter and neighbors talking and children playing doesn't give me the ache in my stomach that shouting and throwing plates does. At home I never saw anyone grab someone in anger, or shove, or yell like Timir yells. People argue sometimes, but their raised voices don't hold the venom of Timir's.

Ne Min picks up a broom.

"Wait, I'll get that," I say, then take the broom from him to sweep up the food and pieces of broken plate from the floor.

"Good thing the elephants leave the river at sundown," he says. "Long ago, I heard of an elephant that was caught in a trap overnight. He was attacked by a tiger."

I glance outside, in the direction of the forest, then look back to Ne Min.

He smiles. "Don't worry, he was all right," he says. "He was a fighter, that one. But most elephants would not be so lucky."

Late at night I lie awake in the stable. I cannot stop thinking about Nandita, stuck in the trap. I didn't want the men to take her out of the forest, but I didn't have a plan for what to do with her. What can I do? In the morning the workers will find her. But what if a tiger finds her first?

It will be my fault. I am the reason she's alone in the trap now and I'm the only one who knows the danger she is in.

I jump up and grab my torch, then light it after checking to make sure the rain has stopped.

The sounds of animals I do not recognize echo all around as I hurry back to the river. I'm thankful I can't see everything that lurks in the night.

As I get closer to the trap, I start to run. Branches scratch my arms and face, but I keep running.

Finally I reach the pit. I kneel at the edge and lean over with my torch. I need to see, but I am afraid of what I will find. The shape of the elephant glows in the light.

"Hey there—are you all right?" I whisper. "I came back, just like I told you."

The wind rustles the tree branches above. Frogs and crickets sing in a chorus around me. I lower my torch into the trap, careful not to touch Nandita. Her back rises and falls with her breathing as she sleeps. I sigh with relief.

I search the area for something that will help free Nandita. My torchlight cannot pierce the thick darkness of the forest, and I stumble over a fallen tree. When I hold my torch close I see that it's a palm tree. It isn't very tall, but it might be wide enough to make a ramp for Nandita. I stick my torch in the ground, then grab the tree with both hands and pull.

It is heavier than I thought. My hands slip off the trunk and I land on the damp ground. The smell of wet earth fills my nose. I stand and plant my feet on the ground to try again. My back and arm muscles strain as I pull. The tree finally slides away from its resting place. Insects and spiders scatter. Something slithers past my feet, and I drop the tree and leap aside. I scan the ground with the torchlight. Nothing. I tiptoe back to the tree, pausing after each step to look and listen for a snake.

Again I grab hold of the tree and drag it toward the trap. Sweat drips into my eyes and down my back, even though the air is chilly. I stop to sit and rest. With only two more steps I will be standing at the edge of the pit.

And then what? Will this even work? My muscles ache as I stand once more to pull the tree to the trap. One step, then two—then the muddy edge of the trap falls away. I cry out and grip the trunk when my feet slide into the pit. The bark scrapes my hands that claw the tree.

My feet try to dig into the sides of the trap. The mud slips away, not allowing me any foothold. Thankfully the tree is too heavy to fall into the trap with me.

Nandita, now awake after my shout, trumpets and bellows her anger. Her trunk slaps at my legs dangling into the pit.

"Look, I don't want to be in here either!" I yell. "What am I supposed to do?" Nandita paces the floor of the trap. She bumps into my feet when she passes beneath me. My hand slips and I clutch the tree tighter. Squinting, my eyes follow the grayness of her back as she circles the inside of the pit. *"Come on, help me out,"* I beg Nandita, or Ganesh, or anyone who is listening.

Nandita walks under me again, and I step onto her back. My arms shaking, I use the last of my strength to push off Nandita's back and lift myself up until I can lay my chest on the flat ground. I crawl on my elbows until I am completely out of the trap. On the ground I rest to catch my breath as I listen to the thrashing, bellowing elephant.

"All right, Nandita, let's get you out of there, too." I ease the dead tree over the opening of the pit. Nandita reaches up her trunk. The tree hovers over the trap. Little by little I slide the tree forward until it touches the other side of the trap. Easing up, I let the end of the tree slide into the pit until the far end hits the ground.

Now that the tree is in the trap next to Nandita, it doesn't look so big. Why did I think this would work?

Even if I get her to step onto the tree, it's going to snap in two under her weight.

I drop my head onto my arms and cry. This isn't fair. She didn't choose to be away from her family to work, like I did. But I don't know what else to do for her.

As I grow sleepy I fight against my drooping eyelids. I pick up a stick and peel away the bark with my pocketknife. A small pile of shavings collects at my feet before the torchlight dies. Finally I fall asleep.

I wake with a start. Branches shake overhead. Something jumps from a tree and lands on the opposite riverbank. I should turn to see what's there, but I sit frozen. Moving only my eyes, I dare to glance across the river.

A pair of glowing eyes stares back at me. I slide my hand to my torch, forgetting it no longer holds a flame. I can make out the outline of a large cat. Not as large as an adult tiger, though. Maybe a leopard? Or could it be a young tiger? Do they attack things that are bigger than they are? Hopefully its mother isn't around. I scan the forest for another pair of eyes piercing the darkness. My hand searches the ground for my pocketknife, even though it will not be of much use if I'm attacked. I don't want to harm an animal, but what if the animal harms me first? Or if it harms someone I care about? I look into the trap again, where Nandita sleeps, then back to the cat.

I force myself to quiet my breathing. The water splashes as the animal dips its paw into the river, then the silver skin of a fish flops onto the riverbank. I sit trembling next to the trap while the animal eats its dinner. Hopefully the fish will be enough.

With one last look, the cat turns and disappears into the darkness of the forest.

My heart's beating so fast, I'm sure it will keep me awake the rest of the night.

But I must have drifted off to sleep, because the sound of a nearby animal startles me awake again. I laugh when I see it is only a peahen, digging in the ground for its breakfast. Sunlight peeks through the trees. I lean over the edge of the trap and see Nandita staring up at me.

"I'm so glad you're all right!" I tell her. "I'll go pick some mangoes for you."

As I rip a branch from the mango tree, I hear another sound in the distance, one as unwelcome as a tiger's growl. The truck from the circus sputters to a stop at the edge of the trees. My heart races as it had when I saw the big cat. I am out of time. Nandita is trapped, and I can't do anything more to save her.

I have not thought how to explain why I'm here, covered with mud, or why the trap now holds an elephant—and a dead tree.

10

What one hundred men will drink in a day, so will an elephant.

—From *Care of Jungle Elephants* by Tin San Bo

A trail from the tree stump to the trap shows where I dragged the tree. As the workmen climb out of the truck I race along the length of the trail and kick leaves over the dirt to cover it.

"What are you doing here?" Sharad asks when he sees me. "Timir is furious that you ran away."

I remember the mouse Timir crushed when he warned me about leaving the grounds without permission.

"I didn't run away." I take my time joining the men at the trap and think about what to say next.

"I woke up early and couldn't get back to sleep, so I decided to come here before breakfast to see if we'd caught an elephant yet." I point to the trap. "This one must have fallen in after I left last night. I was just picking some mangoes for its breakfast." I drop the branch into the pit.

Sharad leans over the trap to peek at Nandita. She pulls fruit from the branch and shovels them whole into her mouth. She holds one mango in her trunk and hurls it at the face peering at her from above. The fruit smacks Sharad right in the forehead.

Sharad curses and rubs the red mark on his head, then backs up a few steps. Too bad for him Nandita didn't hit the top of his head. That mound of piled-up hair would protect him from anything.

He cranes his neck to watch Nandita from farther away as he wipes mango juice from his face. "Well, it's a strong one. Not bad. About two years old. Still young enough to train but big enough to give rides." He pauses. "What's that tree doing in there?"

I do not look at him as I answer. "I was wondering the same thing. I guess it fell."

"Fell?" He looks around. "From where?"

Yes, from where? I look around while I think of an answer. "It did get stormy last night. Maybe the wind blew it in."

"That was quite a wind then." Sharad scratches his head. "Well, Timir will be pleased, finally," he says. "Now, get in the truck." He turns to the workmen. "Let's go get the bigger truck and the chains."

"I can stay here with the elephant," I offer. "To stand guard." Even with all the dangers the forest holds, I feel safer here than with Timir. And I don't want to leave Nandita alone again.

The men laugh. "With the elephant?" says Sharad. "Why? So you can run away again? The elephant isn't going anywhere. Now get in the truck!"

"But I didn't run away, and we should find a way to give her some water. She's been stuck in there since . . ."

"Well, go on," says Sharad. "She's been stuck in there since when?"

"Since who knows how long? We don't know when she fell in there."

"Probably just this morning. She'll get water soon enough. Now get in the truck. The sooner we get out of this jungle the sooner we can get the elephant out of there."

I plod to the truck behind the workmen. With one last look at the trap, I climb into the back.

The men chat with one another on the way to the circus grounds, but I am silent. I cannot stop thinking about Nandita, all alone in the trap again. *Is she safe? Is she scared?*

The truck jerks to a stop. Sharad leaps out of the driver's seat and bolts through the gate toward Timir's office. I follow the other workers and overhear Sharad boasting to Timir in the doorway.

"Great news! I have an elephant for you—and I caught the boy, too, before he could run away any farther."

"What? Run away?" I hurry to the office door. "But I told you I wasn't—"

"What happened to your head?" asks Timir. The lump on Sharad's forehead has turned purple.

"Oh, that's nothing," explains Sharad. "That elephant has quite a temper, but I'll break it of that soon enough."

"Of course. Excellent work. But you"—he looks past Sharad and glares at me—"have earned a fine of one thousand rupees. You know the rules. You are forbidden to leave the grounds without permission. Is that clear?"

"A thousand rupees! But that will take me—"

"An extra three months of work should do it. Now, go get my elephant."

11

A foolish man believes he can trick an elephant.
　　　　—From *Care of Jungle Elephants* by Tin San Bo

I stomp to the elephant truck and crawl into the back. *Three extra months! I was just protecting the elephant!* What will my family think when I don't come back in a year? They won't know what's happened to me. My eyes fill with angry tears when I think about how many days I'll have to work here before I go home.

A bed of straw covers the floor of the truck. Blocks of wood of all different sizes are stacked next to me, and a pile of ropes and chains sit coiled in one corner. The sides of the truck have high wooden walls like thick fences.

The workmen climb into the cab, and the engine

coughs and rattles when Sharad starts it up. The truck lurches and I tumble backward.

When we reach the trap, Sharad gets out of the truck and pounds on the side. "Time to get to work!"

The two workmen hop into the back to collect the supplies. I carry the ropes and chains while the men haul the wooden blocks to the trap.

"Climb in, now. We'll toss the blocks down to you," says Sharad. He hands one of the workmen a rope and tosses the other end into the pit.

"Climb in? With the elephant?" I don't know how to free an elephant from a trap, but I didn't expect that getting into the trap myself would be part of the plan.

"Of course with the elephant, you idiot. You're the smallest one here. Put the steps in place so the elephant can climb out."

I hope this turns out better than my ramp. My hands burn as I clutch the rope and scale down the slippery wall of the trap. Nandita groans and moves away.

"Now, move back—stand next to the elephant," a workman calls when I reach the bottom.

Nandita looked so small when she stood next to the adult elephants. Now that we're together in the trap she seems much larger. The top of her head is as high as my shoulders. She pushes her forehead against my side, and I brace my hand on the side of the trap so she won't knock me over. For the first time, I notice reddish-brown hair that stands up straight on her head and back. With one finger I reach out to touch her head, ready to pull my hand back if it feels like I'm petting a cactus. The bristles of hair are rough, but they do not hurt like cactus needles. What I notice most is that she doesn't look like she's smiling anymore.

The largest block of wood comes into view as the workmen shove it to the edge of the trap. The pile of leaves crackles when it crashes onto the trap's floor. Nandita cries out and backs away from the block of wood.

"Go on," Sharad calls down. "Push it in place to make the first step."

I kneel and push the heavy wood step to the dirt wall. One by one the men drop blocks of wood down to me. Each block for the staircase is smaller than the last, but I have to carry each new step to the top of the stack, then descend the stairs to collect the next one. When I'm close to the top of the trap, the workmen can hand me the wooden blocks instead of dropping them down to me. My arms shake as I stack the last step.

At last I have a staircase fit for an elephant. I crawl from the top step onto the ground and catch my breath.

I look down into the trap at Nandita. "How will we get the elephant to walk on the staircase?" I ask. "Will she understand she has to climb the steps?"

"She'll understand perfectly once we start pulling," says Sharad. "Here." He hands me the chains.

"What do I do with these?"

"Do I have to explain everything? Get back down

there and wrap one chain around the elephant's neck and another around its leg, then connect them with the other chain."

And then what? Nandita is young, but I do not think we're strong enough to pull her anywhere she doesn't want to go. I descend the steps and pat Nandita on the head.

"Don't worry, we'll get you out of here soon." I wrap the chain around her neck and click the latch closed around one of the links. I do the same with the leg chain. When I'm done Sharad hands me a long chain to connect to the chain around her neck.

I climb out of the trap again and notice Sharad looping the other end of the long chain around the bumper of the truck. He orders a workman into the driver's seat.

"Are you sure this will work?" I ask.

"Of course it will work!" Sharad says. "We'll drive the truck to pull her, and she'll climb out."

"But do you think the bumper . . ."

"Now drive!" he yells. The wheels spin and fling mud into the air. The noise of the struggling engine drowns out Nandita's protests as the chain pulls her body. The engine quiets, and the driver leans his head out the window.

"It's not working!" he calls.

Sharad steps behind the truck. "Try it again," he shouts, then turns toward the trap.

"Sharad," I say, "you're right behind . . ." My warning

is lost in the noise of the spinning wheels and the roaring engine. With a *thunk* the bumper breaks free and the truck charges forward. The bumper smacks into Sharad. He lands facedown in the mud.

I run to check on Nandita. "Are you all right?" I ask her. She trumpets and grumbles at me.

"Well, I'm not all right, in case you were wondering!" yells Sharad. "Get over here and help me up!"

I walk to him and hold out my hand. He grabs it and rolls his round body toward me, then groans as he heaves himself up from the ground. Leaves cling to the mud that covers his face and body. It is hard not to laugh—he looks like a giant angry bird.

He storms to the truck and kicks it, then inspects the damage where it struck a tree. Glass from a shattered headlight dots the crumpled front bumper. He uncoils the chain and tosses the bumper into the back, then opens the truck's cab. As he walks back to the trap, the sunlight reflects off the shiny object he clutches in his hand.

"What's that?" I ask.

"It's an elephant hook."

Now that Sharad stands closer, I see the instrument more clearly. The large metal hook curves to a sharp point at the end. I look to Sharad, the question I'm afraid to ask stuck in my throat. *What is it for?*

"Get back down there with the elephant while we pull

on the chain. If she doesn't want to move, a good whack with this will convince her."

I pretend I don't see him holding the hook out to me and hurry down the block staircase. Nandita leans against the wall of the trap.

"Come on—we have to get you out of here!"

Nandita shuffles forward. "That's it, keep going," I encourage her. She bumps into the bottom step. The chain pulls and I push. Nandita lifts her foot and places it on the wooden block. Step by step, with me pushing behind her, she climbs the staircase.

Once Nandita is out, she pushes past Sharad and starts to run into the woods.

"Get back here!" Sharad yanks on the chain and the workmen grab Nandita. She cries out like she did when she fell into the trap. Sharad lets most of the chain drag along the ground so he can hold Nandita close.

"Get the tailgate!" Sharad orders me. I run to the truck and drop the tailgate to the ground to make a ramp.

Nandita sways as she walks to the river. She places her trunk into the water and fills it like a huge straw, then pours the water into her mouth.

Sharad jerks the chain. "Come on!" he grumbles.

The ramp creaks when Nandita steps onto it. She stumbles into the truck, and I crawl in behind her. Both of us jump when Sharad slams the tailgate shut.

"Don't worry," I say as I pet her head. "Someday I will

set you free. I'll be your family until then. I know it won't be the same, but I'll take good care of you. I won't leave here without you, I promise."

And I mean it, too, but I don't feel any better. I feel like a mosquito promising to take back its bite.

12

The elephant calf depends on its mother's care for
three to five years.

    —From *Care of Jungle Elephants* by Tin San Bo

At the circus grounds, Sharad pulls up to the side of the property fence that has a metal gate. The truck fits through this gate easily because it's much wider than the wooden ones behind the cook shed and near the arena. I sit up in the truck bed to peek through the cab's window. A chain loops through the gate's handle and around the fence post next to it. Sharad opens a padlock to release the chain, then pushes the gate open. After climbing back into the cab he drives through the gate and stops next to the arena. One workman jumps out of the truck and waves his hands to guide Sharad through the arena gate, while the other runs back to close the metal gate.

The chain around Nandita's neck drags on the bed of straw as she paces the length of the truck. Sharad parks inside the arena and comes around to the back of the truck.

He releases the tailgate, then holds out his hand. "Give me the chain. Help me get her out of there, then report to the office for your instructions."

I hand the end of the chain to Sharad. It rattles against the tailgate as Sharad runs to a thick wooden pole in the ground and latches the chain to it. The workmen approach the truck and Nandita cowers in a corner. She leans away from the men who pull the chain. I stand behind her as I did in the trap.

"Come on, you didn't want in here and now you don't want out." I try to push her out of the truck, and pray that Sharad won't find a reason to use the hook.

The truck rocks and creaks as Nandita finally moves forward then down the ramp. I follow her out. She backs away from Sharad as he approaches. He slams the tailgate shut and Nandita darts across the arena. She runs as far as the chain reaches, then falls to the ground when the chain jerks her back. The workmen laugh.

Nandita stands up, pulls and struggles against the chain, then runs the other way until the chain stops her again. She calls out with a trumpet blast and wraps her trunk around the chain and pulls. I want to run to her and help, but I only stand and watch her wrestle to break free. The chain does not break. It digs into her neck as she fights and fights. Still the chain does not break. Finally she gives up and lies down in the dirt. The chain lies on the ground next to her.

Come on, you can do it.

I wish she'd stand up, or at least sit up and fight the chain again. Anything to show she hasn't given up so soon.

But Nandita stays on the ground, and I turn to report to Timir's office.

Timir is sitting in his desk chair with his back to me, so he doesn't see me in the doorway. It looks like he's staring at the case of knives mounted on the wall. The knives have matching ivory handles like his cane, but the blades are all different. Some have long, thin blades that end with a sharp point, and one wide blade has an edge like a row of tiger teeth. Another blade is curved with a smooth edge.

With one hand I hold the stone in my pocket, and with the other I knock softly on the open door.

Timir spins his chair to face me. "Good, I was about to call you."

I step through the doorway. From behind his desk he picks up a folded blanket. I catch it when he throws it to me, and I run my hands over the fabric. It's not very soft, but it will be more comfortable than the bed of straw in the stable. Now I'll be able to lie down on one blanket and cover up with another. On cold nights I will wrap myself up like a caterpillar in a cocoon.

"Thank you," I say to Timir. "I have been wanting an extra blanket. And it's huge!"

"It's for the elephant, idiot," he says. "Make sure she stays covered during the night. And when she gets hungry, you will find the powdered milk and the bottles in the cook shed."

"How will I know when she's hungry if I am sleeping?" I ask.

"She'll let you know."

I try to picture myself feeding a bottle of milk to an elephant. While I'm wondering if Nandita will stand in place long enough to drink a bottle of milk, I realize Timir is still giving me instructions.

". . . twice a day. There's a shovel and a pitchfork in the stable."

Pitchfork? Do what twice a day? I'm afraid to ask. I will have to figure it out later.

"Whenever Sharad brings in a truckload of new hay, stack the bales next to the stable. You can use the wheelbarrow to move them. The metal bucket hanging on the trough is for hauling in water from the spring. When the trough is empty, fill it again."

Through the office window I glance at the water trough. In my head I try to count how many trips to the spring and back it will take to fill it. I wonder how fast Nandita will empty it.

"Give her a bath in the spring every evening," Timir continues. "Keep hold of her chain when you lead her around. We can't have her wandering like she's free to go where she wants. She needs to know you're in charge. I think that's enough instructions for now. Any questions?"

Yes, a thousand. I do not dare ask anything else.

"All right, then," Timir says. "You've had it easy so far, with no elephant here. It is time to end this vacation of yours and start working off your family's debt to me."

Start? In my mind I scratch out the seven marks on the stable wall I thought I had earned.

"Now get to work," Timir says.

It takes five trips to the spring to fill the water trough. I head back to the arena, where Sharad is leading Nandita around, holding her chain close. He pulls the chain back when she tries to run from him.

After washing the lunch dishes, Ne Min hands me a glass bottle about the size of my arm, filled with milk. "The elephant will be ready for lunch, too," he says.

"Don't take too long," Sharad says when he sees me approaching the arena with the milk. "She needs to get back to work." He pulls a cloth from his pocket to wipe the sweat from his face, then leaves me alone with Nandita.

She notices the milk as soon as I open the gate. She reaches for the bottle, but I pull back in time to hang on to it.

The rubber top of the bottle looks like part of a cow's udder, so I hold it over Nandita's head for her to drink as she would from her mother. She grabs the bottle with her trunk. The milk dribbles onto the ground as she tries to feed herself. She spins away when I try to take it back. I chase her around the arena, hoping to get her to drink the milk before it all spills. I wonder if it will be this exhausting to feed her every time.

I lead her out of the arena, through the trees and toward the stable to let her get some hay and water. When Nandita dashes toward the trough, I fall to the ground and the chain slips from my hand. She fills her trunk with as much water as it takes me to collect in one trip to the spring. She pours some of the water into her mouth, but saves some to spray onto her back and at me.

"You'll have more water for drinking if you stop playing around with it!" I watch the water sink into the ground.

But Nandita doesn't seem to know I am scolding her. For a moment, I catch a glimpse of that smile she always wore in the forest.

I grip her chain tightly when it's time to lead her back to the arena, but Nandita runs toward the trees, dragging me behind her. She stops and reaches for a mango branch, but I jump up in time to grab the fruit first. Nandita squeaks and reaches for the mango with her trunk.

"Not so fast," I tell her as I back away. "You're going to have to follow me to get this."

We walk to the arena, Nandita bumping into me the

whole way while trying to take the mango. I keep it close to my chest and I turn away whenever she reaches for it. Finally we make it through the arena gate, and I hold out the mango. Nandita snatches it from my hand and runs across the arena before dropping it into her mouth. She swings her trunk and calls out a trumpet sound.

"You're welcome," I say, and slump against the fence to catch my breath.

When I put Nandita in the stable for the night, I decide to go to bed, too. Before I fall asleep, I take out my pocket-knife. I pick out a new log and stab the knife into it, marking my first day of work that matters.

I'm so tired, the bed of straw feels almost comfortable. I have never been so tired. Nandita is not so sleepy. She groans as she paces around the stable and bangs the walls with her trunk. I try to ignore her, but she grabs my blanket with her trunk and walks away.

"Nandita, please," I beg her, "go to sleep." I stand and pick up her blanket. Every time I try to cover her, she walks away from me. I give up and sit on the straw, leaning against the wooden logs that make up the stable walls. Every time I doze off, Nandita's cries and flinging trunk wake me.

"You are more annoying than a camel!" I tell her.

At last she grows tired, too, and lies down. I cover her with the blanket, then collapse onto the straw.

"Good night, Nandita."

I dream that I am so confused about how to care for Nandita that I shovel out the river and fill the water trough with hay. Then I dream that Chanda is a new baby again, crying on her blanket.

"She is hungry, Hastin," my mother says. *"Bring her to me."* When I reach to pick up Chanda, she is gone, but I still hear her cries. Somehow I end up in the forest. Behind the river rocks and in the branches of the great banyan tree I search for her. I lift the broad green leaves of the plants on the ground, but Chanda is not there. I spin in circles, not knowing where to look next. My search becomes more frantic as Chanda's hungry cries grow louder. But how can I hear her crying when she is so far away?

I pry my eyes open to ask Amma for help. In the darkness I look around to figure out where I am. The straw crunches under Nandita's feet as she paces. She cries out and bangs the walls of the stable with her trunk.

"Nandita, are you hungry?" I pull myself up, then pet her on the head to calm her down. The bristles of hair tickle my palm. She stops pacing, but still I hear the cries from my dream.

I run to the cook shed and hope I can figure out how to prepare a bottle of milk. After I light the lantern I find a pail of water and a burlap bag of powdered milk on the counter. Next to the bag is the big glass bottle, over half full with water. Now, how much dry milk to put in? When I pick up a metal cup next to the bottle, I notice it's already full of powdered milk. Silently I thank Ne Min. He must have measured everything out for me before he left.

I remove the rubber top of the bottle and pour in the powder. After I replace the top, I squeeze the end of it closed and shake the bottle back and forth to mix the powdered milk and water together.

As fast as I can I race back to the stable.

"Here, Nandita." I hold out the bottle. "Drink your milk, then let's get back to sleep."

I grip the bottle tightly, but Nandita's able to steal it from me again. Milk spills onto the straw as she tries to place the bottle in her mouth with her trunk. She lets out a squeaky cry when I take the milk from her, but quiets down once it's in her mouth. With a few loud gulps, she empties the bottle. There is no telling how much she really drank. Milk covers her face and my own arms. Between that and what spilled on the ground, I hope she has had enough to keep her quiet for the rest of the night.

I do not bother cleaning up. Nandita lies down and I cover her with her blanket.

On my bed of straw I close my eyes and think about Raj. If Chanda isn't home, there is no one to feed him. Maybe he's moved on to another village, or he's looking for food in the desert. Does he wonder where I am? I hope he doesn't think I abandoned him. I wonder about Nandita's family, too. They must have thought about her when they passed by the trap this evening.

I feel like I have not been asleep long before I am awakened again, this time by Nandita's scream—a scream so full of fright, I am sure there must be a tiger right outside the stable door. I jump up from the bed of straw and light my lantern, then scan the stable for what could have harmed her. The light that sweeps across her face shows me she is asleep.

I remember Chanda wanting me to hold her hand after a nightmare. The bad dreams stayed away then. On a nail overhead I hang the lantern and move my blanket closer to Nandita. I lean back against the stable wall and rest my hand on her back.

Her cries quiet, but her breathing is quick, as if she is still afraid. I stay awake until the up-and-down waves of her sides slow enough to let me know the nightmares are gone for now.

Elephants have strong attachments to their family members.
　　　—From *Care of Jungle Elephants* by Tin San Bo

I wake up to the smell of elephant dung and sour milk. Somehow during the night I ended up facedown in the straw. Nandita paces around the stable. After I stand up and stretch I lean against the wall of the stable and close my eyes. Already I know I will spend the day counting the hours until bedtime.

"I'll be back with your breakfast. Be good," I tell Nandita as I pet her trunk. She tries to follow me out of the stable, so I crack the door open just enough to slip out.

Empty milk bottle in hand, I walk to the cook shed as I pick straw off my clothes and face. Ne Min is already preparing breakfast. He looks up from the dough he is mixing and smiles.

"You look like an old man, like me," he says. "She will not always keep you awake at night. It will take time. She is afraid. An elephant her age, she needs her mother."

"Do they have dreams?" I ask. "Elephants, I mean. Do they dream?"

"They dream, and they remember."

I grab the water tub. "Thank you for measuring the dry milk for me. I would not have known what to do."

"That young, she is still looking for her mother to give her milk. She will grow tired of hay. Pick some fruit and leaves for her, and you will have a friend for life." He takes the empty milk bottle from me and sets it in the tub. "Fill this up while you're at the spring."

When I return with the water, I place the tub on the wood-burning stove to boil, then mix a new bottle of milk for Nandita. This time when I feed her in the stable, I'm able to hang on to the bottle and place the end of it into her mouth. I take her outside so she can eat some hay and drink from the trough. Then I return her to the stable and go back to the cook shed to help Ne Min.

We shape pieces of roti dough into balls between our palms, then place them on the flour-covered countertop. With just a few rolls of the rolling pin, Ne Min makes perfect circles of dough, but mine turn out wobbly and uneven.

"It takes practice," he assures me.

Ne Min cooks the roti with a few drops of oil instead of on a dry pan, so it is crispy instead of soft like the roti I'm used to.

When it's time to season the pot of beans on the stove, I uncap the spice jars Ne Min points to and hand them to him, then he sprinkles in a bit from each one. A dash of turmeric whirls bright orange in the liquid. The dark brown powder in one jar burns my nose as soon as I remove the lid. Ne Min drops the smallest pinch of this spice to the pot. Then he stirs in something that adds both sweetness and sourness to the air.

Timir and Sharad enter the cook shed just as I finish setting the table. Only the four of us are here now—since Timir has his elephant, he doesn't need the other workers any longer.

When the water boils, I remove the tub from the stove and place it on the floor. By the time we finish eating, the water will be cool enough for washing dishes. I am in such a hurry to get to the table that I set the pot down too quickly. My skin turns red where the water splashes onto my wrist. But I am so hungry I ignore the stinging pain.

At the table, my roti is halfway to my mouth when I notice Timir's glare.

The day just started. What could I have done wrong already?

"What do you think you're doing?" Timir says.

Eating breakfast, you dung beetle, I want to say. But I

have learned when Timir asks me a question he does not really want me to answer.

"You've fed the elephant?" he says.

"Yes," I answer.

"And cleaned the stable?" he continues. "The water trough—it's full?" Each question is louder than the last one.

I set down my bread and keep my eyes on my plate.

"Have you not listened to anything I've told you, or are you just too stupid to figure out what to do?"

That is another question I don't know how to answer, so I take my plate to the counter and leave the cook shed.

Holding Nandita's chain, I lead her through the trees to the arena for her training with Sharad.

I realize now that the pitchfork and shovel Timir mentioned in his instructions yesterday are for cleaning out the stable. With a wheelbarrow, I haul the dirty straw far into the trees so the smell won't bother anyone. I grab fresh straw that's next to the trough and carry it to the stable.

When I see Timir enter his office, I return to the cook shed to help Ne Min clean up after breakfast.

"No, you need to eat," he says when I pick up a dish to wash.

"But Timir said—"

Ne Min waves a hand like he's swatting a fly. "Timir is busy in his office now. Your plate is on the stove."

I don't like leaving the dishes for Ne Min, but my

stomach rumbles at the smell of breakfast that still hangs in the air.

"I suppose I'll work better after a good meal."

Ne Min smiles.

With a white cloth I grab the hot edge of the plate and carry it to the table. The circle of roti wobbles on a hill of onions and beans. My plate is fuller than it was before.

"Did you get enough to eat?" I ask Ne Min.

He doesn't look up from the dishes he's washing. "We all had plenty, Hastin."

I hope he's telling the truth, but I don't remember there being leftovers after we filled the plates at breakfast. Sometimes at home I saw mothers and fathers give up food from their own plates if their children were still hungry after dinner. So it's not only the cook shed that makes me feel more at home, but Ne Min, too.

I try to be polite and eat my food slowly, but I'm so hungry that it disappears from my plate as fast as water into Nandita's trunk. Ne Min laughs when I bring my empty plate to the water tub so soon after I sat down.

All I want to do after that big meal is lie down for a nap, but I have to get back to work. I cut enough firewood to carry two armloads to the cook shed.

I make several trips to the spring to fill Nandita's trough and the water tub for Ne Min, then it's time to start preparing lunch.

• • •

That evening after dinner I unlatch Nandita's chain from the post in the arena to lead her to the spring for her bath.

"Take this with you," Ne Min says as we pass the cook shed. He hands me a coconut husk.

"What do I do with this?" I ask.

"It's for her bath. That rough skin, it's uncomfortable. Scrub her with this to get rid of the dry skin. But be gentle with her spine." He touches the bony part of my back.

This time I use both hands to hold Nandita's chain, but it slides out of my grasp when she dashes ahead of me. I chase after her and dive for the chain as it bounces along the ground. I'm able to grab hold of it, but Nandita keeps running, dragging me behind her. She charges into a clump of bamboo. The stalks smack me in the face with a *thwack-thwack-thwack* until Nandita stops to eat.

I push myself off the ground and lean against Nandita until she decides she's had her fill of bamboo. When we reach the water's edge she dips her trunk in the spring, then pours the water into her mouth. She sprays the cool water over her back, soaking me just as much as herself. I'm laughing too much to scold her. The water rushes over her body when she lies down in the spring. I scrub her with the coconut husk. A mosquito lands on Nandita's back, and I leap out of the way as she swats it with her trunk.

I pretend I'm a jungle boy, stopping to rest with my elephant on our journey into the wild. *On the back of my elephant I ride through the jungle. We can travel as far as we want and even climb mountains. In the heat of the day we swim in a cool river . . .*

When Nandita turns over in the water, the rattle of the chain snaps me out of my daydream, and I remember where we are. Not in a jungle home, or any home at all.

14

During the elephant's bath, one should look for wounds or sores that need attention.

—From *Care of Jungle Elephants* by Tin San Bo

Through the clear rippling water of the spring I notice the spot of deep red.

Nandita still lies on her side in the water. When she flaps her ear forward I see what I missed when I scrubbed her. To get a closer look I wade into the water, but she rolls herself to standing and moves away. When I catch up to her I try to hold her and ease her ear forward. She spins around and slaps me on the legs with her trunk. But I had enough time to glimpse the wound. The sore is larger than any insect bite I have ever seen, and deeper.

I grab her chain. "Come on, Nandita, let's get you some help."

As soon as we leave the water, Nandita rolls in a patch of dirt and uses her trunk to spray dust over her back. She looks dirtier than she did before her bath.

Sharad is putting away his equipment in the supply shed when we approach him. "She's hurt," I say. He hardly glances up when I point to Nandita's wound.

"She's fine," he says.

"But—it looks really bad. Should I put something on it? Some medicine?"

"She's just started her training. She'll catch on soon enough."

He is not making any sense. How her training could have anything to do with the sore behind her ear, I don't know.

"Think about it," he says. "You think she can feel anything through that thick skin?"

She felt the mosquito.

I give up on Sharad and lead Nandita to the stable. Through the gaps in the wood I see Ne Min walking toward the small wooden gate I now know leads to the trail to his home. I'm not sure how he knows so much about elephants, but I am thankful to have him to talk to.

I run out of the stable to catch up with Ne Min. "The elephant is hurt," I call to him. "I don't know what happened." He turns and hurries to me.

We enter the stable together and see Nandita resting on the straw. Ne Min kneels down next to her. He holds Nandita's trunk in his hand and blows into the end of it.

Softly he speaks to her in a language I do not understand. Nandita flaps her ear forward and shows him the wound.

"*Tah*," he says as he pats Nandita's side. She stands up. "Good girl." He brushes his hand along her trunk then reaches for my hand.

"How did you learn to speak elephant?" I ask as I help him stand.

Ne Min laughs. "It's Burmese."

"Then how did an Indian elephant learn Burmese?"

"She does not understand the words, but she understands me," he says. "Approach them with respect, and without fear, and they will know what you ask of them." He examines the wound again, then looks away. He winces as if Nandita's injury is his own. Ne Min doesn't just know about elephants, he cares about them.

"Go to the supply shed," he says. "Get the bottle of iodine—the big brown bottle. Also the insect repellent. Then, from the cook shed, some sugar."

"Sugar?"

He nods and turns back to Nandita.

The heavy wooden doors of the supply shed creak open when I pull the handles. My eyes need a moment to adjust to the darkness in the depths of the shed. Shelves filled with boxes, glass jars, and bottles line the three walls, from the ground to the ceiling. I look at several of the brown bottles to figure out which one might be what Ne Min asked for.

I grab a cloth, insect repellent, and what I hope is

iodine, then head to the cook shed. From a cabinet I take the burlap bag of sugar and place it in the crook of my arm. When I return to the stable, Ne Min is still talking to Nandita and petting her trunk. I kneel down to let the supplies fall onto the straw.

Ne Min smiles when he sees the bag of sugar. "Just a little next time. Enough to fill a spoon." He glances at the brown bottle. "Hand me the iodine first, and the cloth."

The white cloth turns reddish brown when he pours some liquid from the bottle.

"Clean the wound twice a day," he says as he works. "Whenever she is injured, take her to a quiet dark place— like this—to treat her." He caps the bottle of iodine and hands it back to me. "After the iodine, a little sugar."

I open the top of the bag, then tilt it just enough to pour some sugar into my hand. I don't want to invite any ants to spend the night with us in the stable. Ne Min nods when I look up at him to see if I have enough. He takes the sugar from my palm and sprinkles it onto Nandita's wound.

"Last, the bug repellent," he says, "to keep the ants away from the sugar, and the flies from laying eggs in the wound."

I cannot believe Nandita stands still for all of this. I hand Ne Min the bottle of insect repellent, which he pours onto Nandita's injury.

"So now you know where to find everything, and how to take care of the sore when it happens again?" he asks.

I nod. "But you think she will get this again?"

"I had hoped not, but I am afraid she will. Many times."

"How did it happen?" I ask, even though I'm afraid to hear the answer that part of me already knows.

"It was the hook," he says. "You have seen the shape of its point, and the shape and depth of her wounds. If you are going to take care of her, and keep her safe—" He looks away. "Sometimes you'll have to see things you don't want to see."

The straw crunches when Nandita lies down again.

"What do you call her?" Ne Min asks.

"Nandita," I say.

He looks at her face. "Not so joyful," he says.

"She was when I named her. See how it looks like she's smiling?"

The old man and the elephant stare at each other. "Her eyes are sad," he says.

So are yours, I want to say.

He takes Nandita's trunk and holds it out to me. "Here, blow into the end of her trunk."

"Why would I do that?" I ask.

"To help her remember who you are. Their sense of smell is strongly tied to their memory."

I do as Ne Min says. He pats Nandita on the back, and she rolls to her side.

"How do you know so much about them?" I ask.

"I am old. I know everything." Ne Min collects the supplies and leaves the stable.

The next day, after I lead Nandita to the arena, she tries to follow me out when I leave.

"No, you have to stay here," I tell her as I pet her head. "I'll be back later." She reaches her trunk across the fence to touch my face. I hate turning away from her, but we both have work to do.

I'm chopping wood when I hear voices coming from the arena. Sharad is working with Nandita, but I recognize Ne Min's voice, too. He is talking louder than he usually does.

"You know there are better ways," he says.

"Like my father's ways?" says Sharad.

"Yes."

"A lot of good that did him."

"That had nothing to do with it," says Ne Min. "What would he think if he could see you now?"

After a long silence Sharad answers, "But he can't."

Twice a day I treat the wound behind Nandita's ear, and a few days later a new one like it appears on her back. The next day as I work I try to find a way to watch Nandita's training and see for myself how Sharad is treating her. I clean the stables, help Ne Min, and paint Timir's office while Sharad works with her. When I carry the water to the cook shed or fill the trough I glance toward the arena, but too many trees stand in the way for me to see what's going on.

While I am in the supply shed, I hear Timir calling me. Maybe if I stay here long enough he'll think I've gone to the spring for water. My heart races. The smooth stone from Baba gives me some comfort while I hide behind some burlap rice bags. When Timir quiets, I crack the door just enough to glance around, then slip out.

One of the trees next to the arena is a tamarind tree, thick with leaves and fruit. If I can climb it, the leaves will hide me from anyone's view. I start to run to the tree, then freeze when Timir sees me. He leans against the arena fence, where he watches Sharad and Nandita. She has her side turned to Timir, but she keeps one eye on him. I've noticed that Nandita stiffens as if she's afraid when she sees Timir or hears his voice.

"Where have you been?" he asks me. "My office needs another coat of paint."

I trudge to Timir's office and pick up the paint can and brush. I'm painting the side of the office when I hear Nandita scream. It is the scream of her nightmare, but worse—sharper. The trees behind me block my view, so I drop the paintbrush and run to Nandita. As I get closer I see that she's running in circles around the arena. Timir's glare stops me. He points toward his office, and I back away.

The next day the hours creep by even though my

chores keep me busy. Just before it's time to help Ne Min with dinner, I look around for Timir. I creep closer to his office. He must be at his desk—I do not dare peek in to check, but I hear grumbling and the shuffling of papers.

I head to the arena and climb to a strong branch of the tamarind tree. I peek through the limbs of the tree to watch Nandita's training. Sharad orders her to walk through a large hoop he holds.

What a stupid trick. No wonder she doesn't want to do it. When Sharad turns, I see the hook in his right hand. I lean closer to get a better look. It seems like Nandita might actually walk through the hoop. She steps forward and lifts a foot.

"That's it—good girl," says Sharad.

Then Nandita spins around, away from the hoop, and slaps Sharad on the bottom with her trunk. I cover my mouth so Sharad won't hear me laugh.

He throws the hoop down. It circles and wobbles before resting on the ground.

Nandita backs away from Sharad when he raises his arm. Then the hook slices the air and punctures Nandita's skin. She screams.

My hands cover my ears and I squeeze my eyes shut.

I do not know how long I sit in the tree. When I finally look up, Sharad has left. Nandita rocks back and forth while chained to her post. I want to comfort her, but when I scale down the tree I run straight to the cook shed.

Certainly I am late in helping Ne Min prepare dinner, but I don't care about that right now.

Ne Min stands at the stove with his back to me.

"I saw him," I say. Ne Min turns around. "Sharad. I saw how he trains her. I know you told me, but it was different, seeing him . . ." My voice feels stuck in my throat.

Ne Min joins me across the room and squeezes my shoulder. "There is goodness in Sharad," he says. He holds up his hand when I start to protest. "You do not believe me because you have not seen it. He has kept it buried for so long, maybe he has forgotten about it himself. But I believe it is still there. The best hope for Nandita is that Sharad will find that goodness back."

My anger, still fresh as Nandita's new wound, does not let me see any goodness in Sharad, buried or not. Ne Min is wrong about this.

15

Dry grasses are easy to keep and long lasting, but will not provide enough nutrition if used as the only food source.
       —From *Care of Jungle Elephants* by Tin San Bo

Now that I've seen how Sharad treats Nandita, I'm careful to take even better care of her. She is my responsibility. Over the next weeks I pay more attention to everything Nandita does. When I scrub her at bath time, I search for new sores. Each time, I hope to find nothing wrong, but I must learn to see things I do not want to see. When she eats, I observe how much. Is it more or less than the day before? Does she seem hungry, or does she pick at her food? I'm not sure what to do if she doesn't eat enough, but I notice anyway.

Whenever I lead her around I hold her chain like Timir asked, even though I don't really need to. Nandita tries to follow me everywhere. She even waits outside the door when I go to the outhouse.

I've learned that she likes to be petted on her trunk and forehead, but not her back. Sometimes when I'm busy working, she nudges me with her head until I take a break to pet her. She also nudges Ne Min when he's nearby. Often he doesn't look at her face when he pets her.

One evening when I feed her outside the stable, Nandita curls her trunk around some hay, then scatters it to the ground like she's not interested in eating. From the woodshed I take the ax and run to a tamarind tree to chop a branch full of sand-colored pods.

Beyond the stable the trees are thicker. From tree to tree I search for more food for Nandita. My eye catches the broad leaves of the mango tree, so I chop down one of those branches, too.

Nandita pulls the mangoes from the branch and drops them into her mouth. While still chewing the last fruit, she reaches out her trunk and grabs the tamarind branch from my hand.

"Nandita, be patient," I say.

One by one she eats the tamarind pods, then she eats the leaves and bark.

I lead Nandita into the stable and decide to sit down to carve something out of mango wood. Everyone else has left for the day, so Sharad and Timir aren't around to bother me about sitting down for a while.

With Baba's knife, I peel away slivers from the piece of wood to round the edges at one end. The other end is jagged where I hacked at it with the ax, so I even it out to make a figure that will stand upright in the stable.

After studying the block of wood, I start carving a face. While I work, I feel my father over my shoulder, guiding me. *Smooth out that area. Even out the eyes. Watch how you hold the knife.*

Yes, Baba, I am being careful.

The figure I carve does not look like the one I pictured in my mind. I imagined the Ganesh I made would look like the one at home, only smaller. But the head is lopsided, and one ear is larger than the other. Baba's carvings were so smooth. I wonder how any pair of hands could make something so perfect. The skin of my Ganesh is bumpy, like a road that would make for a bouncy rickshaw ride. But the eyes I have right—evenly spaced and small, a wise and laughing Ganesh. I set him in one corner of the stable, close to where my head rests at night. He leans a bit to the right, so I stack more straw on that side so he will not worry about tipping over. I hope he does not mind the shape I have made him.

One morning as I'm serving breakfast, Timir asks Sharad, "How soon before we're ready for the show? We need to get started."

"She is stubborn," says Sharad. "She doesn't know all the tricks yet, and I haven't started training her to give rides."

"Then we'll start the show with the tricks she can do. We're not earning any money waiting for her. Work her harder so she'll learn the rest of the tricks faster."

"We have a few things ready. She can do a show in early February," says Sharad.

"Two weeks, then," Timir says. "We need to get the word out now that Circus Timir is coming back. I want you and the boy to start making posters tonight to advertise the show."

Nandita tries to follow me out of the arena after I drop her off there. I reach over the top of the fence to pet her head. I hate to think about what she is going through each day with Sharad. What will it be like now that Timir ordered him to work her harder?

"Be good now, and do what Sharad says."

She touches my nose with her trunk.

What kind of elephant keeper am I? Every day I leave Nandita with someone who hurts her, then walk away. But what can I do to protect her?

After dinner, Sharad stays behind to work at the table in the cook shed, drawing and lettering posters with pencil. When he is finished with a poster I lay it flat on the floor to paint it.

For a long time I don't speak to him. Seeing him brings me back to the tamarind tree where I watched him hit Nandita with the hook.

But it isn't fair to Nandita to keep quiet. Sharad didn't listen to Ne Min, so he probably will not listen to me, but I have to say something. There are still too many new wounds.

The poster I've painted of an elephant kicking a ball is finished, so I set it aside to dry.

When I look at Sharad, I see the hook, and hear Nandita's screams.

"I don't want you hurting the elephant anymore." I barely hear myself speak. It's hard to talk when it feels like a python is squeezing my chest.

Sharad stops drawing and turns to me. "What did you say?"

I take a deep breath and try to sound braver than I feel. "If you are a good trainer, you can find a way to teach her without the hook."

Sharad leaps up from his seat and steps toward me. From my spot on the floor he towers over me.

"What do you know about them?" he yells. "You haven't lived with them all your life, you haven't seen—do you know what they're capable of?"

I back away when he grabs the elephant hook from his belt. He steps closer to me and waves the hook in my face.

"You have to show them who's in charge!" He turns away and slams the hook into the table, stabbing it with its point. He leans forward and rests his hands on the table, like he needs to catch his breath.

I try to think of something to say, but nothing seems

right. Sharad looks like someone who needs to be comforted, but I cannot tell him it's all right, because it isn't. And I can't say things will get better, because I don't know if they will.

Again he says, "You have to show them who's in charge," almost too quietly for me to hear him this time. He pulls the hook out of the table and walks away, leaving an unfinished poster.

Timir spots me as soon as I leave the cook shed. I'd like to hide or pretend I don't see him, but it's too late.

"My office needs cleaning," he says before he walks away.

There is so much paper to go through, and I am so tired. I don't even know what to do with most of Timir's things. The crumpled papers on the floor I suppose can go into the trash bin. Does he realize he has a trash bin? There it is, right next to his desk, but it seems he never uses it. With a clean cloth I wipe away the layer of dust from the furniture.

The sofa is threadbare in spots and sags in the middle, but it is comfortable when I sit down on it. I will rest my eyes, just for a moment, before I get back to work.

I fade into a dream about Chanda on Amma's lap, laughing as she plays her game of dropping her doll onto the floor for me to pick up. As soon as I brush off the dirt and hand it back to her, she lets it fall again. This time when I reach for the doll, it turns into a snake, coiled and ready to strike.

Even as I sleep, I hear the *step-click-step* of Timir's approach. From the depths of my dream I scream at myself, *Wake up!* but I can't. Finally I pry my eyes open, just in time to see the cane hurtling toward my head.

"I come back to check on you, and this is what I find. Sleeping on the job. You've just earned yourself three more months here. You must want to stay here with me for good."

It's the middle of January, but it's the fullness of the moon that tells me of the passing months, not the marks on the stable wall. I still scratch a line on the wall each night but I have stopped counting them, since I no longer know how many days I must stay here. Timir added time to my service when I spilled straw from the wheelbarrow and forgot to pick it up, and when I left the paint can on the ground after painting his office.

If I could one day say, "Look, Nandita, one hundred marks. If I do that three more times, I can go home," that would be helpful. Or if I could ever celebrate the last mark in a row of scratches across the wall and think, When I do that twice more, it will be time to leave, the tracking of my days would make sense. But I do not know when I will carve the last mark or where it will fall. Still I make them. I feel I must do something to measure my time here.

Tonight Nandita falls asleep long before I do. She wakes when a distant rumble of an elephant herd breaks the silence of the night. She stands up, flaps her ears, and calls out to them.

I wonder if it's her own herd. "I know, I miss my family, too," I tell her.

Finally the faraway herd quiets, and so does Nandita. She lies back down and drapes her trunk across my stomach.

Next to my Ganesh figure, I pray for both of us.

"Ganesh, wise son of the goddess,
You who begin all good things
Grant me your blessing
Of freedom from fear."

But I wonder if anyone is listening, and if I will ever break free from this dark place.

16

Elephants find ways to amuse themselves.
  —From *Care of Jungle Elephants* by Tin San Bo

The first show day draws near, and our work has no end. I did not think it was possible, but Timir is even more demanding than he was before. And Nandita still wakes up twice a night for a bottle of milk, so I feel like I am sleepwalking as I work.

Thankfully Nandita has eaten the grass that grew in the arena, so that is one less area I have to clear. But I do have to make an area for cars to park.

Timir put up the posters in the town nearby to advertise the elephant show. Two days later he went back to talk to tour bus drivers and hotel owners. But his eyes look worried, and his nervousness has rubbed off on all of us. Sharad has grown tired of Timir's questions—he would never say so out loud, but I can tell by the way he rolls his eyes when Timir is not looking.

"The hoop trick—she can do it now?"

"Yes," Sharad says each time. "Perfectly."

"And the game? How is she doing with the game? What about the box? Is it ready? It's strong enough for her to stand on?"

The morning of Nandita's first show arrives. Finally we will be able to sit down and watch the performance we have worked so hard for. After I fill the water trough, I look around for any last chores to do before the show. Ne Min steps out of the cook shed and calls to me to bring firewood.

I'm stacking the wood next to the stove when I hear the hum of an engine. Ne Min and I peek outside, then I run toward the arena to see the tour bus that bounces into the drive.

Our first visitors file out. They line up across from Timir, who sits at a table with a sign that reads "Rs. 25." He collects the twenty-five rupees from each person, then places the money in a metal box. Some of the people look around the circus grounds and say "What is this place?" and "We asked our driver to take us shopping. Where are we?"

With a wide smile and a laugh, Timir welcomes the visitors to his circus and assures them they won't be disappointed. His friendliness reminds me of the first time I met him in the café—the Timir who bought me samosas and tea and convinced me to take this exciting job.

He invites the customers to sit on the wooden benches. The two lowest benches are close to the arena, just high enough for the audience to see over the fence. Behind those are two more rows of benches, elevated a bit more so the people who sit there can see over the heads of those in front. Last is a fifth row, higher than all the others.

Two taxis and a hotel van bring more people to the show. I notice that the people who rode in the taxis and vans pay their admission, but the drivers do not. Instead, Timir slips some money to each driver when he greets them at the table. *He's paying them to come to the show?* The drivers join the audience and step to the back row to take the last empty seats.

Just before the show starts, I carry a small bench from the cook shed to the arena fence, then sit down to see if we'll be able to see the show from here. The bench isn't high enough for me to see over the fence, but if I look between the logs I have a good view of the arena. It would be easier to watch while standing at the fence, but Ne Min might get tired. I run back to tell him I have a place for him to sit during the performance.

He's cleaning the stove and doesn't look up. "I cannot go, Hastin. I will stay here."

"But it's Nandita's first performance. She's been working so hard. Don't you want to see her?"

"Not today. I cannot see her today." Something in Ne Min's voice tells me not to say anything more, like a scorpion with its raised stinger that warns, "Don't come any closer."

I trudge back to the arena and sit on the bench alone. While I wait I keep glancing back toward the cook shed, hoping Ne Min will change his mind and decide to join me. For this first show, I don't know what to expect. How will Nandita behave, and how will Sharad react if she doesn't perform like he wants? The worry that churns in my stomach would calm down if Ne Min were here. I reach for my pocket and realize that Ne Min reminds me of my stone—old and small but strong, and I feel safe when he's nearby. I think he has a story, too.

I wonder where Nandita and Sharad are and if I should check on her. I try to look through the trees to see if I spot her near the stable. Out of the corner of my eye I catch the shuffling walk of Ne Min's approach. Without a word he takes his place next to me, and I let go of the stone.

We turn toward the audience when a little girl shouts, "There it is! There's the elephant!" The audience members crane their necks and look across the arena.

Sharad struts alongside Nandita toward the arena gate. He wears an outfit that I guess used to fit him at one time. Gold buttons strain to hold his red jacket closed.

The puffy white collar and ruffled sleeves of his shirt stick out from beneath the jacket. Over his white pants he wears knee-high black boots. He seems quite proud of himself. I have never seen anything so ridiculous. Is this what Timir meant by "clowns"? He said they dress funny. I hold my hand over my mouth to cover my laughter.

Sharad smiles and waves a gloved hand at the crowd— then trips over a branch on the ground.

Oh no. I should have made sure the path to the arena was clear. After all our work day after day, I cannot believe I did something so stupid. Perhaps he will catch himself, and no one will notice.

But no, the crowd gasps as Sharad falls flat onto the ground. It wouldn't have been so bad if he hadn't cursed so loudly when he landed. My stomach tightens when I hear the *step-click-step* of Timir and his cane. I do not have to turn around to know he's standing right behind me.

"See me in my office after the show," he says.

Sharad stands up and brushes dirt from his clothes, then opens the gate and leads Nandita to the center of the arena. He holds her chain close, but she leans away from him as if she doesn't want to get any closer to him than she has to. They stand in front of a wooden box painted in bright colors.

"Up," Sharad orders. Nandita climbs onto the box.

She looks scared, like she wants to run away. I wish I could stand with her and pet her forehead to comfort her. Sharad clutches some palm leaves in his hand and slides them along Nandita's head and back.

"I've never seen him pet her with palm leaves before. Does she like that?" I ask Ne Min.

"Look closer," he says.

When Sharad moves his arm, I notice a bit of the silver handle he hides in his sleeve.

"He tied the palm leaves around the hook so he can hold it without anyone knowing?"

"Yes," Ne Min says. He nods toward Nandita. "But she knows." Certainly she feels the cold hook through the palm leaves when Sharad brushes them along her back.

Ne Min looks down and I put my hand on his shoulder.

The audience claps politely when Nandita follows Sharad's commands to raise her trunk or her feet. A few people look around the property, like they're wondering what else there is to see here. Timir waves his hand to signal Sharad to move on.

"Down," Sharad says. "Sit." More people clap when Nandita sits on the wooden box like it's a chair, her front feet out in front of her. Sharad takes a piece of fruit from his pocket and gives the treat to Nandita.

She performs a few more tricks: she waves her trunk when Sharad instructs her to "Say hello," and she stands on her hind legs. Nandita waits in the center of the arena while Sharad walks toward me. I do not notice the hoop until he picks it up from where it leans against the fence, right in front of our bench. He walks to Nandita and holds the hoop in front of her, then points to the center of the hoop with the leaf-covered hook.

"Step through," he says.

Nandita does not step through. She stands in place.

"Step through," Sharad orders again. He holds the palm leaves behind one of Nandita's front legs. The people in the audience shift in their seats. I glance at Timir where he stands next to the fence. He clutches his cane so tightly the color of his hand matches the ivory handle. Splinters dig into my fingertips where I grip the edge of the wooden bench.

Finally, Nandita raises her foot. Sharad points again to the center of the hoop. Nandita ducks her head and steps one leg after another through the hoop. The crowd applauds, then cheers and claps louder when Sharad points the palm leaves at the ground, prompting Nandita to take a bow.

Sharad gives Nandita her treat, then steps forward to take a bow himself. Nandita circles away from him and raises her trunk.

Don't do it.

Nandita slaps Sharad's bottom. The laughter of the audience grows louder. Sharad spins toward her, his hand raised. He glances at the crowd, then lowers the hook. Again, he holds the hoop and orders Nandita to walk through it. Nandita snatches the hoop from Sharad's hand, then runs across the arena, holding the hoop high with her trunk. The audience roars with laughter as a yelling, red-faced Sharad chases Nandita. When he catches up with her, he grabs the hoop and throws it to the ground. He holds the palm leaves behind Nandita's leg and leads her back to the center of the arena.

After he catches his breath, Sharad announces, "Now for the last event of the show . . ." He ignores the disappointed groan from the audience and rolls a ball out from underneath the wooden box. Some children in the audience jump up from their seats and stand close to the fence when they see the ball.

Sharad sets up a sawhorse on either side of the arena. The one on the far side has a flat elephant-shaped piece of wood nailed to it.

He drops the ball to the ground and dribbles it from side to side with his feet, then passes it to Nandita. The crowd cheers for her as she runs with the ball in front of her toward the sawhorse marked with the wooden elephant. Sharad runs alongside her. I don't know if Nandita really means to run the ball into the goal. Maybe Sharad just trained her to run to the sawhorse, and the ball is propelled forward by the force of the lumbering elephant behind it.

When she is close to her goal, Nandita stops running. She walks up to the ball when it comes to a rest, then kicks it so it rolls under the sawhorse. The audience laughs and applauds for the first point of the game. Sharad gives her two pieces of fruit, then retrieves the ball. Nandita runs next to him as he kicks the ball across the arena.

The audience claps when Sharad kicks the ball into his goal, but not as loudly as they did for Nandita.

After they each score one more point, Sharad again passes the ball to Nandita. The crowd grows noisier as she approaches her goal. Just before Nandita can kick the ball into her goal, Sharad steals the ball from her. A disappointed "Awwww!" rises from the crowd when Sharad makes a long kick across the arena to score another point for himself.

Nandita walks, head down, to the center of the arena. Perhaps she is just disappointed about missing out on more treats, but she seems sadder than that, as if she somehow knows she lost the game. Sharad picks up the ball from his goal, then joins Nandita.

"Not a bad player for a little elephant." He pats her head. "Thank you all for coming to the show. Please come again, for you will enjoy—"

Nandita's trunk knocks the ball out from under Sharad's arm. She steps behind the ball and runs again toward her goal. The audience stands up to cheer when she scores another point.

She jogs back to the center of the arena. Sharad tries to smile but looks sick to his stomach as he and Nandita both take a bow.

We wave goodbye to our departing visitors until the last vehicle drives out of sight. Then Sharad rips the palm leaves from the elephant hook and turns toward the arena. Timir grabs his arm after his first step.

"Where are you going?" he asks.

"To teach that elephant a lesson," says Sharad.

"You'll do nothing of the kind. That was perfect."

"What? She ruined the show—she made a fool out of me!"

"What she made is a lot of money for us. The crowd loved it. Some of them will come back, and they'll tell others to come. And when they do, you will perform the show the same way you did today."

After cleaning the arena, I go to Timir's office like he asked. He was so happy about the show, I have some hope that he will not punish me too harshly for not picking up the branch. I hear voices as I approach the office, so I wait outside the door while Timir talks to Sharad.

"People were asking for elephant rides," says Timir. "How soon can we offer that?"

"I'll have to train her, and she's too small to carry an adult yet," says Sharad.

"Get the boy to help you then."

"Maybe when she knows her other tricks better. Right now there isn't time—"

"Your father could have done it," says Timir. "Too bad he's not around."

Sharad says nothing, and the shuffling of papers tells me that Timir has turned back to the work on his desk.

Sharad clears his throat and speaks again, but his voice

is so quiet I have to lean closer to the doorway to hear him.

"I suppose I could find some time to practice," he says. "About the boy, though—I'd rather not work with him."

With Timir's next words, I shiver as if facing a gust of wind on a rainy night.

"You might as well get used to him. He's here to stay."

17

On cold nights, elephants huddle close to their young to keep them warm.

—From *Care of Jungle Elephants* by Tin San Bo

It is near the end of winter, and my hopes have faded like the sun.

People spread word about the funny elephant show, like Timir said they would. Nandita performs three times a week, each time to a full audience. Still, Timir isn't happy—the show's success has made him greedier instead of satisfied. He adds extra shows to the schedule, and we are all overworked. Nandita especially.

After each performance, Sharad calls me to help train Nandita to give rides. She's gotten better these past few weeks, but it took a long time for her to get used to having someone on her back. When I first climbed on she ran in circles until I fell off. She allows me to stay on now, but it's still a bumpy ride.

Sharad throws a blanket onto Nandita's back and secures it with a rope, then commands her to kneel onto her front legs. I climb up and hang on to the rope as she walks around the arena. When she speeds up to a jog I have to lean forward, ignoring the scratchiness of her hair on my face, and cling to her neck so I don't fall off.

Sometimes I have to drag her to the spring for her bath, and it's harder to wake her each morning. I would do anything to help her, if only I knew what that was.

Nandita seems nervous, too. She startles easily when she hears a loud noise, and rocks herself back and forth in the arena. A circular rut is worn into the ground where she paces around the wooden post.

One thing is better: my chores have become easier as the months have passed. When I haul water from the spring, the tub seems lighter every day. I fill it just as high as before, but I travel faster and no longer have to stop and rest on my way back to the cook shed. Chopping wood is easier, too. My arms have grown larger, and the ax is not heavy in my hands like it was when I first arrived. My hands are now tough with calluses. "You are growing like a bamboo stalk after a monsoon," Ne Min tells me. I wish he were right. I feel like Timir will always tower over me.

I wonder how I will ever get home, and what I will find when I get there. My stomach bunches into a giant knot when I think about how long I'll have to wait before I see my family again.

Thoughts of escape are with me every day. Sometimes during a show I think, Just run away. Leave the stable at night and don't stop walking until you're home. Then I argue with myself, But I promised I'd work here.

And what did Timir promise? Adventure! One year of service, when he never meant to let me go.

Another day I might be filling the water bucket at the spring, and the voice that is braver than I am jumps in again: What about now? If I walked away now, how soon before they'd notice I was gone?

But what would happen to my family? I'm working to pay Timir back for Chanda's medicine and hospital stay.

And what would happen to Nandita? I promised I wouldn't leave here without her.

Late at night I lie awake in the stable, my head throbbing. Long after I forget the reason Timir hit me again, the pain still lingers. With my fingers I trace the shape that the handle of Timir's cane left on my forehead. I've done enough for him. When the time is right I will go. But when will that be?

I take the stone from my pocket. Once I asked Baba how the stone ever got out of the river where it tumbled around for so long. He didn't know the answer to that.

Then one evening just after everyone has left and there's still a little light in the sky, I stop fighting with myself.

Instead of pushing aside the thoughts of leaving, I ignore the reasons to stay. I lead Nandita past the arena to the property fence and the large wooden gate. We'd leave through the wide metal gate if only it weren't closed with a thick chain and padlock. Maybe Nandita can fit through this one.

I walk through the gate ahead of Nandita. She pauses and looks at the gap left by the open gate like she's not sure she'll be able to pass through it. I'm not sure either, but we don't have another way out.

"Come on, let's get out of here." I tug Nandita's chain to coax her forward.

The fence creaks and groans as she squeezes through the gate. Flecks of bark, scraped free from the wooden posts, drift to the grass. A tight fit, but Nandita makes it. We're outside the circus grounds.

We run along the fence line until we reach the path that leads to the river. Our first stop will be the forest where I last saw her family. They must wonder how she's doing. Will they still be there? I don't know if elephant herds move around or if they keep their homes in one place. But there's nowhere else to take Nandita.

Which way will I go after I leave her in the forest? I stop to look around, then close my eyes to think. I remember the blinding sunlight the morning Timir drove me away from my home.

When I open my eyes, I find the last orange glow of the sunset. My home will be that way.

We continue walking toward the river. Now and then I glance at the place the sun sets each night, at times pointing to it, so I will not lose it as the sky grows dark.

The farther we walk and the darker and colder it gets, the more I wish I had a better plan. When I exhale I see my breath in front of me, white like smoke. I am running to the wilderness with nothing except the clothes I wear, a pocketknife, and a trained elephant on a chain.

Now what? We're at the river where Nandita used to come with her herd. If they were here before, they've already left for the evening. Maybe they're close enough to hear Nandita if she calls to them, but how can I make her do that?

I unlatch her chain and drop it to the ground.

"Go on," I tell her. "Go look for your family."

Nandita touches my face with her trunk. I kiss her forehead and wrap my arms around her neck.

"Goodbye, Nandita." When I pet her head, the bristles of reddish-brown hair tickle my hand. "You are free now. Both of us are. Remember your friend Indurekha, who looks like moonlight through the clouds? You will play in the river tomorrow like you used to."

Then I know I have to walk away. As long as I am with Nandita, she has no reason to call out to anyone. Sadness fills me up at the thought of leaving her alone and afraid. I hate feeling that I'm abandoning her, but this is the only way she'll blast that squeaky trumpet that will call her family to her.

Nandita reaches her trunk to the tree above us and struggles to grab a branch. I hold the limb down while she pulls a mango from the branch and drops it into her mouth.

As she chews the mango I take the end of her trunk into my hands and blow into it.

"Remember me," I tell her, then I turn and run.

Something behind me snaps a branch and rustles the leaves. I glance back to see what it is, then fall to the ground when Nandita bumps into me. The chilly dampness of the forest floor seeps through the seat of my pants.

"Nandita, what are you doing? Stay here and wait for your herd."

She reaches out her trunk and touches my nose as I push myself off the ground.

If only I could make her understand. With one hand on her back, I lead her to the banyan tree. How can I leave her here alone and go back to my village? She's small for an elephant and in danger of a tiger attack. But I cannot take her with me. The desert is too dry for her. At daybreak we will follow the river until we find her family. Nandita lies next to me as I lean against the tree.

To help keep Nandita warm, I gather leaves into my shirttail and pour them onto her back. Most of them slide off, so they don't make much of a blanket. I hope the leaves that do cover her will give her some warmth. From all around, I scoop leaves toward us to shield us from the cold. I huddle close to Nandita.

I shut my eyes and think of all the things a person should have with him if he decides to escape into the forest with a young elephant in the wintertime. Blankets. An ax to chop down leafy branches. I could use them to make a shelter, or we could lie under a pile of them to keep warm. Food. We have fruit here in the forest, and Nandita has plenty of leaves to eat, but a bowl of rice would taste good to me right now. And samosas. Mango pickle, straight from the cooking pot. A piece of roti. The steam would warm my hands as I held it. While it was still hot, I would pour on the buttermilk.

A torch. I could make a fire if I brought a torch with me. Or even some matches. I fall asleep thinking of the clay stove in our village courtyard, how warm it is to sit near in the wintertime. On the coldest days I would hold my hands against the sides of the stove and move them away only when I felt like they would burn.

Sometimes, just before I wake up, I forget where I am. As I float through that mist between asleep and awake, I think I'm back at home and Chanda is well. I cling to that moment for as long as I can. At times the remembering is like a stab or a bite, when all at once I realize where I am and all I'm missing. But sometimes the truth settles onto me like dew on a forest leaf, giving me time to feel the roughness of the straw and hear the sounds that do not belong to the desert before I think, Oh yes, I am here, at the circus near the forest. Not at home. And maybe Chanda is all right but maybe she is not.

"I'm awake," I say aloud, because it feels like someone is shaking me to wake me up. When I pry my eyes open I still feel the shaking, but no one is here. I touch Nandita's back, where my head rested until a moment ago. Her body shivers as she sleeps.

I stand and pick up her chain.

"Come on, Nandita," I say through chattering teeth. She looks up at me when I try to rouse her, then lays her head back down.

"No, we have to go back." I shake her harder. If anything bad happens to her it will be all my fault. I loop the chain around her neck, then pull it as I walk a few steps.

What will I do if she won't stand up? The only one at the circus I trust is Ne Min, but even if I found his house and woke him, I don't know how he could help. Maybe Nandita would listen to him, but it would take him so long to get here. Walking all this way in the cold would be hard on him, too. Then I would be responsible for a sick old man and a freezing cold elephant.

Again I take a step back and pull the chain. With a groan Nandita finally stands. I lead her out of the forest to the place that holds us captive, but it is the only place that will keep us safe tonight.

I never thought I would be so relieved to get back to the circus grounds. I close the gate behind us and run ahead of Nandita to grab our blankets from the stable. I rush back to her and put one blanket on her head and one on her back. She follows me into the cook shed and lies down on the floor while I light a fire. I'm so cold I want to crawl right into the oven.

Before we go back to sleep I make a bottle of milk for Nandita.

The flames glow in the darkness and melt the chill on our skin. Soon I hear Nandita's soft snoring, but as exhausted as I am, I cannot sleep. I set the empty bottle on the counter, then pick up a small piece of wood from the woodpile next to the stove and begin carving. *For you, Chanda, for whenever I see you again.*

Just as I smooth out the ears, Nandita turns her head to me and opens her eyes. She reaches out her trunk and curls it around the newly carved figure. She lays her head back down and falls asleep again, holding on to the wooden Ganesh like a child with a new doll.

"All right, Nandita." I laugh. "You keep that one. I'll make something else for Chanda." I yawn and lie down next to her, and the two of us sleep on the floor in the warmth of the fire.

I wake to the sounds of a rattling truck engine.

"Wake up, Nandita! Back to the stable—hurry!" I scramble to grab our blankets and rush Nandita to the stable as Timir parks his truck. Ne Min is just getting here, too—I spot him walking up the path from his house. I don't think he sees me.

On my way back to the cook shed I hear the angry voice of Timir.

"Look at this mess! Wood chips all over the floor! Didn't you and the boy clean up last night?"

"Yes, I am sorry," answers Ne Min. "I should have swept again after he brought in firewood. I'll do it now."

"Never mind, start breakfast." He sees me when he turns to leave. "You have work to do," he says as he brushes past me.

"Ne Min, I'm sorry about the wood chips," I say when Timir is out of sight. "I will tell him—"

"Shhh." He slips my pocketknife into my shirt pocket. "Such a cold night, wasn't it? A good night for a fire."

18

An elephant separated from its herd will try to find its way back.

—From *Care of Jungle Elephants* by Tin San Bo

The days start to grow warmer and longer, and for the first time in months, I count the marks on the stable wall. When I reach one hundred, I carve a long line on the wall to mark my place so it will be easier to count next time. I count the row of marks beyond the long line and realize I've been here almost half a year.

My hair falls into my eyes as I stand, and my fingers get stuck in the tangles when I try to brush it back with my hands. It's grown past my shoulders now and is always in my face as I work. At home Amma would cut our hair with her sewing scissors then throw the hair outside into the wind. In a shrub near our home I once found a bird's nest with black hair woven in with the twigs and brown leaves.

In the supply shed I find a pair of shears. With one hand I gather my hair, then with the other I reach the shears back and snip the hair off.

Outside, the wind blows toward my home. I hold up the handful of hair and release it to a gust of wind and watch it fly away. I dream that the wind is strong enough to carry it all the way to my village, where it will help make a nest for a bird. And Amma will see the wavy black hair woven into the nest and know that I am all right.

Again I plan our escape. This time I will be ready. I will not endanger Nandita this time by leaving on impulse. One evening after her bath, I place an empty iodine bottle under the straw in the stable. The bottle is large but light and has a lid to hold the water inside after I fill it. Near the forests there will be plenty of water, but rivers and streams will be hard to find once I enter the desert.

My pocketknife is with me always. When it's time to leave I'll have to grab the ax on our way to the property fence. Nandita barely fit through the wooden gate last time, and she's grown since then. But if I chop away at the fence post next to the metal gate, I'll be able to free the gate from the chain that holds it closed.

Each day as I work and each night as I sleep, I dream of home. I imagine feeling dry sand again and seeing smoke pour from our courtyard stove in my village. I dream of the baking roti and of the buttermilk calming its steam. And my mother's whole-face smile.

I long to hear the mooing of our cow, play ball with Raj, and even look forward to seeing a camel again. Most of all, I need to know if Chanda is all right.

One morning I throw off my blanket and sit up in a panic when I realize it was the sunrise that woke me, not Nandita. I slept all night long. She always needs a bottle of milk during the night, but she did not wake up.

I reach over and touch Nandita's head. She opens one eye and looks at me, then closes it and starts snoring again. I sigh with relief, then laugh.

"No bottle at night anymore?" I say. "I guess you're growing up, Nandita."

Ne Min isn't in the cook shed when I place the water tub on the stove, so I sit down to work on a wooden elephant I've been carving. I don't expect to be as good as my father yet, but after all this time and practice, my skills should have improved more. This figure is better than many I have done—it is smooth and even, and anyone looking at it will be able to tell that it's an elephant. But still, something is wrong, something is missing . . .

Ne Min shuffles into the cook shed and leans over the table to see my work. "That looks like it was carved by someone who has never seen an elephant," he says. "Maybe by someone who has seen an elephant only in a picture. Do you ever see them standing so still?"

"No, but, Ne Min—this is a block of wood. Of course it is still."

He crosses the cook shed to the stove. "And that is why it looks only like an elephant-shaped block of wood. You are thinking of them as carvings with no life. When you focus instead on the living, moving animal, your work will show that."

I close my eyes and think about the first time I saw the elephants. *Stomping through the forest, playing in the river, spraying water from their trunks—those always-moving trunks, reaching for mangoes, ripping down branches . . .*

When I open my eyes I look at the carving in my hand. Lifeless. Ne Min is right, certainly there has never been an elephant that stood so still. Not just still but straight, as if planted in the ground. And the trunk—it lies there like a dead snake. Maybe if I add some curves to it later it will look more like it's moving. I fold the blade of my knife into the handle and drop it into my pocket with the wooden elephant.

After breakfast Timir and Sharad talk at the table while I wash the dishes with Ne Min.

"I'm going to town tomorrow morning," says Timir. "I will be here in the afternoon. But start working on some new tricks with the elephant."

Without Timir around, Sharad will not bother showing

up for work very early. If I leave, it will be a long time before anyone notices. *Tomorrow morning. Tomorrow, before the sunrise, we will leave.* Only when Ne Min nudges me do I realize I have paused in my dishwashing. I sit frozen in place, holding a plate and dishcloth over the water. I glance at Timir as I continue my chores and notice his glare. I smile at him. *Fine, stare all you want. I'm washing your breakfast dishes for the last time.*

That afternoon Ne Min appears at the stable door as I am cleaning.

"I went home to get a gift for you," he says. He holds out a colorful cloth bag.

I prop my pitchfork against a wall. "A gift? Why?"

"I've had this for a long time. I do not need it anymore." He hands the bag to me. I run my fingers over the designs of red, purple, and blue stitched into the canvas fabric. The edges of the black handle are frayed, and the seam along the bottom has been restitched with different colors of thread. The bag looks old and worn but strong.

"Maybe you could make use of it," he says. "It is still good and can carry many things, if you ever need something like that."

"Thank you, Ne Min." I cannot look him in the eye, but I step forward to hug him. I wish I could talk to him more, find out how he knows so much, why he is so good with Nandita, and what makes him so sad. I inhale the smell of cinnamon and pepper and those spices I never knew before I met him. I breathe them in deep so the scents will tie him to my memory.

After dinner I fly out of the cook shed as soon as I finish cleaning. I can't wait to get through my chores and pack my things in the bag Ne Min gave me. I slow down when I see Timir standing outside his office with Sharad. Casually I walk to the stable and keep my eyes on the ground.

I loop the chain around Nandita's neck to lead her to the spring for one last bath. Her ears flap as she dashes out of the stable. She seems to know something important is going to happen.

"One more night, Nandita," I tell her. Tomorrow we will be free.

I close the stable door behind us and wonder what my family and neighbors are having for dinner. Chanda will save a bit of her food for Raj if she is there.

We take only a few steps before Timir's voice stops us.

"Wait," he says. "Something for the elephant."

Nandita stiffens, her ears flat against her head.

I turn to see Timir and Sharad walking toward us. Sharad carries two metal shackles, joined by a thick chain. He kneels down to place the cuffs around Nandita's front legs. With one snap of the shackles he locks away any hope we had of escaping.

19

An elephant will sacrifice its own well-being for the good of the herd.

—From Care of Jungle Elephants *by Tin San Bo*

I stare at the metal shackles that encircle Nandita's legs.

Timir steps closer, and Nandita turns to face him.

He stares at me as he speaks. "I see flight in her eyes. We have to do what we can to keep her here. We'll also be locking the entrance near the arena when we leave every night. It would be a shame if she got out and ran off. Imagine how she would be punished when we found her. Or we'd have to catch another elephant to bring back. Perhaps the elephant has a sister"—he brushes my cheek with the back of his hand—"who would work out just as well. Maybe better."

My face feels like it's crawling with spiders. I back away from Timir's touch and stand closer to Nandita.

Timir narrows the distance between us and raises his cane. Before he can move any closer, Nandita calls out a trumpet blast. Branches overhead shake as the birds that rested in them fly away. Ears flared out straight, Nandita steps toward Timir and throws her trunk across my body.

We all stand frozen in place. Timir and Sharad do not take their eyes off Nandita. Sharad's hand grips the handle of the hook at his side. Nandita stares at Timir with a look I hope she never gives me. Our breathing is the only sound I hear. The silence in the trees adds to the stillness.

Leaves rustle as Timir takes one step back and waits. When Nandita doesn't move, he takes another, and another, holding his cane out in front of him.

"Let's go," he says when he steps just past Sharad. Sharad does not move. "Come on, we're done here for now." He taps Sharad's leg with the tip of his cane.

Sharad shakes his head as if someone snapped him out of a daydream. He joins Timir and backs away from Nandita. She stands in place until they are out of sight. I let out a deep breath I've been holding and slump against Nandita. My shaking hands and pounding heart need some time to calm down.

Nandita has shown before that she cares about me—she crosses the arena when I walk by, even when I don't have a bottle of milk. She likes to sleep next to me, and looks as if she's smiling when she sprays water on me or taps me on the shoulder. But I didn't know she would put herself in danger to protect me. I hope I can do the same for her one day.

I hug her and pet her forehead, then we walk together to the spring.

To make the elephant show more entertaining, Sharad trains Nandita to do harder and harder tricks, like balancing on a row of milk bottles. Even when the show is over, her work is not. After each performance, people from the audience now line up for elephant rides. Nandita kneels onto her front legs for each person to climb on her back, then walks them three times around the arena.

On show days, I let Nandita enjoy a longer evening bath. I scrub her with the coconut husk until my hands are too sore to move, then I sit on the bank of the spring while the cool water flows over her body, which I know must ache.

I imagine myself years from now, as an old man, still sitting here at this spring while Nandita takes her bath. How big will she be then?

Nandita's chains rattle against her shackles when she rolls to her other side in the water. At this moment, she does not look like the sad, overworked show elephant, but more like the playful wild elephant she was when I first saw her. When she looks up at me, her face reminds me of our Ganesh figure back home. Sometimes I used to sit in front of it and listen to the stories my father told. One of my favorites was about how Ganesh got his head.

"He did not always have the head of an elephant, you know," Baba would say.

"He didn't? What happened?" I asked each time, even though I had heard the story a hundred times before.

"Ganesh used to have the head of a regular boy, like you, until the day his father returned . . ."

"Skip to the ending, Baba," I said, "where Ganesh's parents meet the elephant . . ."

"What good is a story if you hear only the end? You have to know how you got there!"

So I would listen while my father told the whole story.

The goddess Parvati was lonely, since her husband, Lord Shiv, had been away from home for so long. So she gathered some earth in her hands and created for herself a son. She named him Ganesh.

One day Parvati told Ganesh, "I am going to take a bath. Guard the door for me, and do not allow anyone to enter. I do not wish to be disturbed."

"Yes, Mother," said Ganesh.

On this same day, Lord Shiv returned home from war. When he tried to enter his home, he was blocked by the boy guarding the doorway!

"Move aside," Shiv ordered him.

"My mother is taking her bath," said Ganesh. "No one may enter our home right now. Come back another time."

Lord Shiv shoved the boy aside and tried to step into the house, but young Ganesh leaped in front of the doorway and would not let his father pass. Shiv was so enraged, he grabbed his sword. He cut off the head of Ganesh and threw it far into the woods.

Parvati heard the commotion outside and ran to the door. When she saw what had happened she cried out, "That was our son!"

The horrified parents ran to the woods to search for Ganesh's head, but could not find it. Knowing their child could not live without a head, they decided to take the head of the nearest creature they found.

The first animal they saw was an elephant. When Shiv and Parvati told him what had happened, the elephant bowed his head and said, "Lord of the World, cut off my head quickly. I will gladly sacrifice it and move on to my next life, so that your son may live."

Lord Shiv told the elephant, "You will not need to live again in this world. I bless you and set your spirit free, so that you may join the gods."

Ganesh's mother and father raced back home with the elephant's head. Shiv placed it on his child's body. Parvati placed her hands upon Ganesh, and their son awoke.

As I remember the end of the story, I think of the animal that was so generous he gave his own life to save another. I look into Nandita's eyes and know that she would do the same if asked. And I would do it for her.

That evening after I finish my chores, I'm looking

around for a piece of wood to carve while Nandita eats hay in the stable. I notice Ne Min sitting on the ground outside the arena. A large roll of brown twine sits on the ground next to him.

"What are you making?" I ask as I approach.

"That elephant, she does not give you room to sleep." The roll of twine unravels in a blur as he works. Row after row of knots appear, each a perfect copy of the one before it. I sit down across from him.

He is right. Nandita has grown so much during our time together. Many mornings I can feel the pattern of bark imprinted on my face, from sleeping while pressed against the stable wall.

"Hang this hammock in the stable and sleep above her. Then she can have the whole floor to herself."

The knots of the hammock seem complicated, but Ne Min ties them in neat rows with no more effort than it takes him to stir a pot of rice.

"You must have made many of these," I say.

"A few. I prefer sleeping mats woven from palm leaves, but you have no room for that. Someone who has his own hut, with an elephant that sleeps outside among the trees, can sleep on a mat and blankets on the ground. But for you, for now, a hammock."

"Some people let their elephants sleep outside? Not locked in a stable?"

"They like to wander around, yes, but if they are treated well, they come back when they are called." Ne

Min smiles and pauses in his knot tying. "The mischievous ones try to hide so you have to look for them, but still they come back." He looks at me, then down at the hammock, and continues working. The roll of twine uncoils even faster than before. "Nandita would return to you, even if she were allowed to wander."

"Maybe. But I'll never know, since Timir would never allow that."

"Timir is one who does everything out of fear."

I laugh. I have never thought of Timir being frightened of anything. He seems so strong, and so scary himself, what could he be afraid of?

"One who is brave inside does not have to use fear to control others," he says. "You are braver than Timir will ever be."

"Brave? Me? I'm afraid all the time!"

"It is not weakness to feel fear. To do the right thing even when you are afraid—that is bravery. It saddens me that I have not always done so."

I try to find the words to ask Ne Min what he means, what it is that bothers him so much.

"Can you tell me—" I start to say.

The swaying of trees in the distance catches my eye. Ne Min turns to follow my gaze. The tops of the trees shake, even though there is no wind. Neither of us moves.

Then I see it emerge from the woods. It is the largest animal I have ever seen.

20

Elephants grow six sets of teeth during their seventy-year life span.

      —From *Care of Jungle Elephants* by Tin San Bo

If one man stood on the shoulders of another, he still would not meet the eyes of the elephant that stands before us now.

As he walks closer to us, he pulls up clumps of grass with his trunk. He beats them on the ground, then places the grass in his mouth when enough dirt has been pounded away.

"If Nandita ever grows that big," I say, "there won't even be room in the stable to hang that hammock. I'll have to sleep outside."

"She will not grow to that size, even if she does live to

be as old as this one," says Ne Min. "The females do not grow as large as the bulls."

"He is old?" The bull looks so strong, like he could crush a truck if he stepped on it. "How can you tell?"

Ne Min points. "See the pink face? And the ears—look how tattered they are, and how they fold."

The elephant is still far away, so I don't know how Ne Min noticed it so easily, but I see it now. The edge of the animal's ear is raggedy and flops inward. Splotches of pink cover his face and trunk.

"That means he's old?" I ask.

"That, and those tusks. You see—that one he has broken, perhaps in a fight, but it takes many years to grow tusks that size."

Each tusk looks thicker than both of my legs put together. "I wouldn't want to meet the elephant that dared to fight him."

We both stand and watch the bull as he pulls grass and ambles toward us. He's not close enough to touch, but I don't want him to get any closer.

The air around us is quiet. Timir and Sharad have gone home for the evening, so we hear no shouting from Timir, no yelling demands of Sharad's training. The only sounds are of the bull pounding grass on the ground and the chewing as he eats. At times he looks at us, then wraps his trunk around another clump of tall grass he yanks from the ground.

In a quiet voice I ask, "Is he as old as you are?"

"Not that old, no," Ne Min answers. "If their teeth could last longer, they could live to be as old as I am. This one may not have many years left. He might have wandered all day looking for grasses that are easy to eat."

"Their teeth wear out?"

"You have seen how much Nandita eats every day. Imagine how all the chewing of hay and grass wears down their teeth, year after year. Like your wood carving, only much slower. When you whittle away at the wood, bit by bit, there comes a time when there is nothing left to work with."

"So it's like their food whittles away at their teeth."

"It takes a long time, but yes. By the time they grow as old as he is, most of their teeth have worn away. They die when they can no longer eat."

"And then what?"

"And then they are dead, Hastin."

"Yes, but—" I have never mentioned to anyone that I wonder sometimes about Baba. He must have been re-born by now into someone else, somewhere else, but I wish I knew who, and where. I would find him and visit him, even if his new self would not know me.

"What do you think happens to them after they die?" I ask.

"Or after we die?"

"Or that. Do you think they, or we, are born into an-other animal or person?"

"Perhaps." The way Ne Min says "perhaps" sounds like "perhaps not."

"What do you think happens then, if not that?"

Ne Min sits down again and continues working on the hammock. "You know where I keep the candles, in the cook shed?"

"Yes."

"Bring me two."

I do not know what Ne Min is thinking or why he needs candles. The lantern burns brightly enough for this time of evening. But I run to the cook shed and bring back two candles for him. He sets one on the ground and tilts another into the lantern flame. After it ignites he hands it to me then returns to tying knots of the hammock.

"Now what?" I ask.

"Now we wait."

I hold the candle while I wait for whatever it is Ne Min wants me to wait for. The bull elephant still wanders nearby. I remember when I first watched Nandita and her family at the river. During all those trips to the forest, I never did see an elephant alone.

"I wonder where his herd is." A pool of wax collects just beneath the candlewick, then overflows and drips onto my finger.

"When they are a few years old, the bulls leave the herd and live on their own. It is the mothers and aunts who stay together as a family with the young ones."

In all the conversations I have had with Ne Min, I've never found out how he knows so much about elephants. He must have lived around them and worked with them for some time. What kind of circus is this, where the cook knows more about elephants than the trainer and cares more about them than the owner? And me—I'm supposed to be the elephant's caretaker, but I would be lost without Ne Min here to answer my questions.

"So before you came here," I ask, "like when you lived in Burma, were you a cook there, too? Or did you have some other job?" The wax has cooled on my fingertip. When I lift it off with my thumbnail I see the whirled lines that mark my fingers.

"Your candle will die out soon."

I didn't see him glance away from his knot tying, but sure enough, I check my candle and see it has burned almost down to my fingers. Ne Min picks up the candle from the ground next to him. He holds it out between the two of us.

"Time to light mine," he says.

Dots of wax leave a trail in the dirt as I lift my candle to Ne Min's. The wicks touch, and the flame of one candle lighting another burns bright.

"Now blow out your candle," Ne Min says.

I move my candle away from his and blow it out. Black and gray smoke swirls away from the wick.

"No more life in your candle, but mine lives because of it. Is my flame the same as the one you had?"

"Not the same, but it came from mine."

"Yes. Without the light of your candle, mine would have no flame. Your candle has died, but gave light to a new one."

"So when you die . . ."

"What has kept me alive will give life to something else. And soon"—Ne Min points his candle to the old bull elephant, who wanders away from us now—"what keeps him alive will breathe new life into something else." Ne Min blows out his candle and hands it to me.

I don't want to think about Ne Min dying someday, and how lost I would be.

"I should go clean the stable," I say, even though I've already cleaned it this evening. I leave the candles lying on the ground and walk away.

Ne Min comes into the stable with the finished hammock and hands me two metal hooks to screw into the ceiling. I climb up the logs of the stable wall.

After I hang the hammock, I pull on it to test its strength while still clinging to the wall. I roll into the hammock and hang on as it swings above Nandita. I don't know how she will react if I fall on her, but I'm sure she would not like it. Ne Min tosses my blanket to me. The hammock is comfortable once it stops swinging. I peek through the knots at Nandita. She looks up at me, her swinging trunk clutching the wooden Ganesh I carved in the cook shed.

I remember something now that Ne Min said when we first saw the old bull elephant.

"Ne Min, when I asked about the elephant's size, you said Nandita would never grow that big, even if she did live as long as he has. Why did you say 'if' she lives that long? She will live to be an old elephant one day, won't she?"

He opens the stable door to leave. "Not if she stays here."

21

A frightened elephant has the strength of many.
       —From *Care of Jungle Elephants* by Tin San Bo

My eleventh birthday comes and goes, but I feel much older. I try not to think about home so much, but I can't help wondering if Amma celebrated my birthday somehow. I've also given up hope about leaving, and my sadness makes the days seem longer and longer.

Then in late August Timir mentions the new circus.

"I have wonderful news," he says.

I'm almost finished with the breakfast dishes, but I wash the last pot over again while I listen.

"Another circus owner, Ravi Kapur, has approached me about needing an elephant act."

He looks like he's about to leap out of his chair with

excitement, but the rest of us are quiet. I imagine Sharad and Ne Min are thinking the same thing I am: what does this mean for us?

"Where is his circus?" Sharad asks.

"About a two-hour drive . . ."

Toward home or away from it? I want to ask. Water drips down my arm as I hold the pot still.

". . . east of here," Timir finishes. *Away from the sunset. Farther from home.*

"He has all the supplies he needs, a big elephant barn, even a doctor to take care of all the circus animals. All he needs is a trained elephant."

Sharad asks, "So . . . he has a circus, and all the equipment, but no elephant act yet?"

"He did have an elephant. He needs a new one. Kapurji will come here in two weeks to see the show—so it must be perfect. Increase her training time if you have to."

Nandita is so tired at the end of each day, I don't know how she will make it through an even tougher schedule.

"He's willing to pay a lot of money for an elephant that is trained and ready to work. And her trainer, of course."

Sharad's shoulders relax as he exhales.

Ne Min is wiping off a counter that already looks clean. I wonder what will happen to him.

"Will he need the elephant's caretaker?" Ne Min asks.

"Or a cook?" I ask.

Timir looks from Ne Min to me as if he just realized

we were in the room. He stares at me when he answers Ne Min's question. "The boy stays with me. I paid for him, and my circus will need workers."

My heart sinks to the floor. I don't want to stay here without Nandita.

"And what about your circus?" Sharad asks. "If you sell the elephant—"

"With the money from Kapurji, I can start over with some new acts. I plan to bring on clowns, a team of acrobats, and some trained monkeys for now. All of them are less trouble than an elephant, and cheaper to feed." He laughs.

After all this time and so many shows, Timir has never been able to add any new acts. He blames Nandita for costing him too much money in food. How did he not know she would need hay, and lots of it? If Timir had to do the work himself, nothing would survive. I wouldn't trust him to take care of a dung beetle.

I put away the clean dishes and walk to the arena to check on Nandita. She holds her chain in her trunk and bangs it against the post. The deepening rut in the ground shows that she has been pacing in circles again.

I wonder what kind of man Ravi Kapur is. Nandita sways back and forth, and I pet her trunk to calm her down. If he does buy her, it sounds like she will get better care—a barn fit for an elephant, and an animal doctor.

But I can't stand the thought of living here without her. Being with Nandita is what gets me through the day.

I promised her I would set her free one day, that I would never leave here without her, but what will I do if she leaves here without me? Then it occurs to me that if Nandita is sold to the circus without me, nothing will keep me from climbing over the fence at night and running away.

Sharad jogs toward us from the cook shed to unchain Nandita for her training. His smile tells me that he likes the idea of having a new boss.

When I go to get Nandita for her bath, she is not chained to her post like she usually is by now. Sharad is still training her.

"I need more time," he says when he sees me. "She must learn how to walk on her hind legs by the time Kapurji comes." I don't think Sharad will have any luck, when Nandita seems almost too tired to stand on all four legs.

"Will you let me know when you're finished so I can take her to the spring?" I ask.

"Timir thinks it will be funny if the elephant follows me around on two legs, like she's imitating me," he says. Sharad doesn't look like he finds the idea all that funny.

I leave them to go work on my other chores. After I clean out the stable, I chop firewood and stack it next to the stove in the cook shed.

Sharad has not come by to let me know that Nandita has finished her training session, but they must both be exhausted by now. I decide to check on how she's doing and find out if Sharad is almost finished.

When I enter the arena, Sharad is nowhere in sight. Nandita is lying on the ground, chained to her post and shackled. I unlatch her chain from the post. Usually she is the one who leads us to the spring, but now she will not even stand.

I pet her head and trunk. "Come on, Nandita, bath time." Gently I tug on her chain to encourage her to stand. When she still doesn't move, I sit next to her and pet her side as I talk to her.

Finally she stands, but she is wobbly on her feet. She lags behind me while I lead her to the spring. Ne Min's face wrinkles with worry when we pass by the cook shed.

Nandita lies on her side when we get to the spring, and I decide to let her stay here as long as she wants.

She sighs as the cool spring water rushes over her body. When I scrub her, I feel her throat rumble as she growls—not like an angry tiger, but like a purring cat. An enormous purring cat.

With both my hands I pet Nandita under her jaw. Something doesn't feel right—one side seems swollen. I'm ready to jump out of the way of Nandita's slap when I press the area, but she doesn't react. It must not be painful, but I will keep an eye on it.

In the morning I awake before Nandita and decide to let her sleep in. No one else will be here for a while, and she needs her rest.

Smoke pours from the cook shed's chimney. When I enter the shed I see Ne Min sitting at the table, reading a book. I don't smell anything cooking, but a fire burns in the oven and a metal bowl of food sits on the counter.

"Ne Min, why are you here so early?" I ask. He closes the book and moves it aside. Before he slides it away from the lantern light, I see a picture of an elephant on the cover.

"Bring me a stone. A large one, but one you can carry in both hands."

I have no idea why Ne Min would need a large stone, but he will explain himself when he is ready.

Ne Min is standing at the counter stirring the bowl of food when I return with the stone. He opens the oven door. I expect him to take the bowl and place it on the grill over the fire, but instead he takes the stone from my hands and places it directly into the flames.

"What have you noticed about Nandita?" he asks.

I look at the oven before answering, wondering why someone would want to cook a stone. "She is tired, more than she usually is. Even at bath time I have to drag her to the spring, and she's not easy to drag. She slept through the night and is still asleep now."

He hands me the bowl. "Rice and bananas may help her regain her strength. Rest would help most of all, but . . ." He trails off. "What else is different about her?"

163

"I'm not sure, but when I was bathing her, it seemed like her jaw was swollen."

"You're right, it is swollen."

"It doesn't seem painful to her."

"No, but uncomfortable. A sign of overwork." He removes the stone from the oven with a pair of metal tongs. He sets it on the counter and wraps it in a thick white cloth, then places it across the bowl I'm holding.

"A hot compress will help the swelling go down. Hold it for a few minutes on each side," he says.

Nandita is still listless when I see her in the afternoon, even though I have added the bananas and rice to her diet. Throughout the day I reheat the stone and wrap it in the cloth to hold against her swollen jaw. Sharad sighs like he's annoyed whenever I interrupt Nandita's training, but he doesn't say anything. He has to know she needs better care. I cannot imagine how he'll make any progress training her when she can hardly stand.

While cleaning the stable I decide I will try to talk to Timir. He'll probably just yell at me, but if I can convince him that the show will be better if Nandita is well rested, maybe he will listen. He is so excited about Kapurji's visit that he cannot see what is happening right in front of him.

On my way to Timir's office I feel like a sandstorm is raging in my stomach.

I stop outside the office door when I hear voices.

"She's overworked. She can hardly move," Ne Min says.

"Sharad has ways of getting her to move when it's showtime," says Timir. "She can rest at night, like everyone else."

"She must have a break from the work, at least for a couple of days," pleads Ne Min.

"Don't you understand? Kapurji is coming here next week. If the show is not perfect—if he is not impressed—he will not be interested in buying that animal."

"He will be less impressed with an animal that falls down in front of him. If she is not properly cared for—"

"Yes, we know how *properly* you take care of elephants, don't we?"

In my mind I see Timir's face, his eyes cold but his mouth curling into a smile. "You are lucky I let you anywhere near my elephant."

What is he talking about? I couldn't keep Nandita alive day to day if not for Ne Min. I hold my breath while I wait for him to defend himself.

I don't hear him walk away from Timir, so Ne Min startles me when he steps out of the office. He does not look at me as he walks by.

Before I go to sleep I check on Nandita. The swelling under her jaw seems to have gone down a little. I pick up the stone and the cloth to prepare one more compress for the night.

165

In the cook shed, I find Ne Min reading again. If he knows I'm here, he doesn't show it. After I relight the fire and place the stone in the oven, I sit down across from him.

Each page Ne Min looks at has drawings of elephants. As he reads, I scan the handwritten pages for a letter I recognize. Baba taught me a long time ago how to write my name, but I don't see any letters like those.

"I've never seen writing like that before," I tell Ne Min. "It looks like a lot of loops and circles."

He rubs his eyes. "Bring me two leaves. I will show you why."

I run outside and pick two palm leaves, then bring them back to Ne Min. He lays a leaf down on the table in front of me, then hands me his pen.

"Write something on your leaf."

I start to write my name, but as soon as I make the first straight line, the leaf tears.

Ne Min takes the pen from my hand. "Long ago, before they had paper, my people wrote on leaves." He writes on his leaf, using letters like those in his book. "Letters with straight lines, like yours, will tear the leaves." The letters dance across the leaf as he fills it, row after row.

"But rounded lines—not so harsh," he says, "and will not harm the leaf."

I want to find out what Timir meant by his comment to Ne Min earlier, but I'm not sure how to ask.

"Ne Min, thank you for talking to Timir today about Nandita. I know it did no good, but . . ."

"You must find a way to get her out of here," he says. "Yourself, too."

"I tried that before. I don't know how it's possible now, with the shackles." Even if I could get past the fence and escape with Nandita, she could not live in the wild with shackles on her legs. She wouldn't be able to run from danger or keep up with the herd. The metal cuffs, snug around her legs now, would dig into her skin as she grew if no one were around to unlock and loosen them.

Ne Min stops writing and sets the pen next to his leaf. "It complicates things, yes. But you are her caretaker, and she cannot be taken care of here."

"But she will be sold to Kapurji's circus soon. She'll get better care then."

"We do not know that. Timir said he used to have an elephant. What happened to it? He never said."

That is true. I hadn't thought about why Ravi Kapur needs a new elephant.

"Even so," Ne Min continues, "better may not be good enough. She needs to be free."

I cling to the hope that Ravi Kapur will be a kind man who runs a good circus. The best circus, maybe. Even better than Timir's used to be.

"Do you know what happened to Timir's circus?" I ask. "Why was it shut down? Timir says it was the best."

"He is right," Ne Min says. "Always a full crowd, but

167

still Timir was not satisfied. He got greedy and started a new business that would make him even richer." He turns a page in his book, and I see a drawing of an elephant pulling fruit from a tree.

"What was his new business?" I ask.

"Tiger poaching."

"Tiger poaching?"

He nods. "He hired people to hunt for tigers at night. He sold their skins, their teeth, whatever else someone wanted, out of his office. What was left he threw into the bear and lion cages."

"Why at night?"

"Because they're easier to catch, and it's easier to hide what he's doing. Timir does whatever he has to do to get what he wants—a tiger skin, a boy to work for him, or a baby elephant. And he knows how to pay people to pretend to not see what he's doing."

"So what happened? He was caught?"

"Yes, he was. The circus was closed down, and Timir spent time in jail. Not as much time as he deserved."

"How did he get caught?"

Ne Min stops reading and looks me in the eye. "Someone who cares very much for animals must have reported him."

"Does Timir know?"

"If he did, that person would be in the same spot as the tigers, instead of reading a book." He looks like he's holding back a smile.

Finally, I find out a little about Ne Min's past. This must be where he learned so much about elephants.

"You worked for him then! I bet you were his elephant keeper, right?"

"No, I took care of the other animals. Not the elephant. Sharad was the elephant keeper, and his father was the trainer."

"Sharad's father was the elephant trainer? Was he mean like Sharad?"

"No, Kiran was a kind man, and a good trainer."

"He didn't use the hook?"

"His hook was no sharper than my fingers, and he used it like it was meant to be used—not as a weapon, but as a guide." He reaches across the table and wraps his hand around my upper arm. "Like taking someone's arm to show him which way to go."

"Didn't he teach Sharad anything?"

"He taught him well—how to care for the animals, to train them with respect."

"But Sharad isn't like that."

"He was, at one time. Now he acts out of anger. Out of fear, too, like Timir."

"Why? What happened?"

Ne Min closes his book and rests his hands on the cover. He stares out the window.

"One morning a lion escaped from his cage. He ran toward the arena just as Sharad and his father were leading the elephant, Anju, to the stable. As soon as Anju saw

169

the lion, she panicked. Kiran tried to control her, tried to calm her down, and pushed Sharad aside to protect him. But Anju was a full-grown elephant, and more important, she was scared. Sharad stood by the fence, helpless, while the elephant trampled his father."

"Kiran died?"

"Yes, and so did Anju, soon after. Timir ordered her killed, even though she was only trying to run away from the lion, and even though she was sorry. She and Kiran loved each other like you and Nandita do. After the lion was returned to his cage, and after Anju calmed down, she tried to revive Kiran. She lifted him with her trunk to sit him up, and charged at anyone who approached. It was nightfall before I was able to take her to the stable. I stayed with Anju that night, but her crying kept both of us awake."

I think back to my first night with Nandita, when she paced around the stable and cried for her family.

"After that," Ne Min continues, "Sharad was full of anger. He wanted Anju killed more than anyone did, even though his father never would have wanted such a thing. Hard as I tried, I could not convince Timir to spare her life. He got a new elephant soon after that, and Sharad stayed on to be her trainer. That's when he sharpened the hook. He blames all elephants for the death of his father. I think, too, he was afraid the same thing would happen to him. He lashed out at the new elephant, as if to hurt her before she could hurt him."

"After everything Timir did, you agreed to work for him again. Why?"

"When Timir came by to tell me he was starting his circus again, I told him I wasn't interested in working for him. Then he told me he had hired Sharad and would be trapping an elephant soon. I thought of the elephant, away from its family, living with Timir and Sharad, and I couldn't stay away. And I wanted to meet the new keeper and make sure he would treat the elephant well."

"I'm so thankful you did come back," I say. "I wouldn't know how to take care of Nandita without you."

"You would have figured it out, with time. As soon as I met you, I knew I had nothing to worry about. Some people have a heart that connects with the elephants, and some do not. But you and Nandita do not belong here any more than the tigers did."

My finger traces a crack in the wood, made when Sharad stabbed the table with the hook so long ago. Ne Min is right, we don't belong here, but how does he think I'm going to free a shackled elephant?

I look up when I remember Timir's snide remarks about Ne Min taking care of elephants. Could it have something to do with Anju?

"Ne Min, when Timir ordered the elephant killed, who—I mean, did you—did he make you—"

As soon as I see Ne Min's face I wish I could take back my question.

171

"You must know better than that by now," he says. "No one could make me hurt an elephant, ever."

"So what Timir said earlier, in his office—"

Ne Min closes his book. "It has been a long day, Hastin," he says. "We should both get to sleep."

From my hammock I peek through the spaces between the stable logs. Even though I can't see anything but the night sky, I pretend I can see all the way to my house. I picture my mother as I last saw her, when I looked out the back window of the truck to see her standing in the road.

Just before I fall asleep, Ne Min comes into the stable. When I sit up I see that he's holding a palm leaf and a hammer.

He holds up the leaf. "I meant for you to keep this," he says.

"Why? What does it say?"

"It is from a prayer." Ne Min holds the leaf on the wall in front of me and places the end of a nail against it. "It says, 'May those frightened cease to be afraid, and may those bound, be free.'"

With one strike of the hammer he pounds the nail into the wall.

22

What an elephant feels, it feels deeply.
　　—From *Care of Jungle Elephants* by Tin San Bo

In two more days Ravi Kapur will come see Nandita's performance. The good thing is, Timir is so focused on impressing him that he has canceled all shows until then so we can work to make that show perfect.

The work and the heat have exhausted us, Nandita most of all. As much as possible I take her to the spring to allow her to cool off and rest. I notice that she has hook wounds not on her back or her head, but on places that are harder to see, like her belly or the inside of her legs. Timir asked about the swelling under her jaw. His concern surprised me until he said, "We can't have her looking unhealthy for Kapurji."

Each day I still use the hot compress on her jaw. It helps at the time, but she is always swollen again the next morning. I've grown tired of standing in front of the oven. The cook shed is hot enough day to day, but lighting the fire more often to heat the stone makes it unbearable.

It is time for Nandita's training again, but she needs to rest. I must talk to Sharad, even though he probably will not listen. But maybe he would welcome the rest, too, after training her in the hot sun day after day.

Nandita looks back at the stable as I lead her to the arena. If she decided to break away from me and go take a nap, I wouldn't be able to stop her. Either she does not realize this or she is too obedient to try.

"Good, you're here," says Sharad when we enter the arena. "She needs to get to work."

"Actually, I think she should skip this session. She doesn't feel well." I try to sound sure of myself, the expert elephant keeper advising the trainer about the animal's condition.

Sharad looks around, then takes me by the shoulder and pulls me closer. For the first time I notice I am taller than he is.

"Don't you understand?" he says. "This is our way out. Not just for me. Think about her." A flailing arm points at Nandita. "I know she's working hard now, but that will be over in a couple of days, and then she can rest."

Nandita swings her trunk from side to side.

Sharad grabs both my shoulders now. His round face

174

is close to mine as he speaks, his eyes desperate. "This next show has to be the best performance we've ever had. You think I like this? That I want to do this? That I want to bake out here in the sun, training an animal to make me look like a fool? This is all I know how to do. I have a family to take care of—did you know that?"

"No." I never imagined anyone marrying Sharad.

"With five children."

For sure I cannot imagine that.

"I understand," I say. "But I'm worried about her. She is tired all the time now."

Sharad sighs and puts his hands on his hips. He steps away from me and looks at Nandita.

"I think she is fine," he says. "But I'll let her have a short break. She walks on her hind legs pretty well. We do need to run through the performance later to make sure it all comes together just right."

This is the best offer I will get from him, so I nod and lead Nandita away from the arena.

After a long drink at the trough, Nandita enters the stable and flops onto the straw with her wooden Ganesh figure in her trunk. I go to the cook shed to talk to Ne Min.

He doesn't look up from the onion he is chopping when I walk in.

"Sharad is letting Nandita rest for now," I say.

"Good," he says. "I hope it will be enough."

"Two more days."

He says nothing, just chops the onion into smaller pieces on the counter.

"You know, you should ask Kapurji about being an elephant keeper."

"No, that is not the job for me," Ne Min says.

"But maybe you could get a better job with Kapurji."

"I do not need much. My house here is enough, and I will stay."

The night before the show, I cannot sleep. I keep thinking about leaping over the fence and running home. It will be strange not sleeping right near Nandita. I'll sleep more soundly, away from her snores, but that won't make me miss her any less.

I climb down from my hammock and sit next to Nandita. It seems so long ago that I first slept here, right next to her. So long ago that I carved the Ganesh she holds with her trunk. I pet her head and talk to her about tomorrow.

"Nandita, I know you've been working hard," I tell her. She opens one eye to look at me, then closes it. "But you will be away from here soon. Just one more show. Then you'll have a better place to live, with a nicer boss . . ." Even though I have not met Kapurji, he must be nicer than Timir. ". . . and a big barn for you, and better food, I bet, and more people to take care of you."

My voice catches in my throat, and I lay my head on Nandita's side.

"So do your very best tomorrow." I try to sound brave so Nandita won't know anything is wrong, but my voice is shaky. "Make it the best show you have ever done."

She opens an eye to look at me again when I sit up. I cannot be sure she understands me, but I think she does.

The morning of the show, I'm filling the water trough when I hear a car engine. Timir steps out of his office and hurries to meet the white car coming up the drive.

That must be Ravi Kapur. I dump the rest of the water into the trough and run to the cook shed.

"Do we have any tea made?" I ask Ne Min. He pours a steaming cup from a kettle and hands it to me.

"Be careful," he says as I hurry away.

The tea sloshes over the sides of the glass and burns my hands. I want to run to meet Kapurji and hear what he and Timir are talking about, but I force myself to slow down so I don't jostle the tea glass anymore.

Already I hear Kapurji's laughter, the loud belly laugh of someone who enjoys laughing often. Timir must have said something really funny, as unlikely as that seems. Sharad exits the arena and joins them.

The men stop talking and turn to me as I approach. Ravi Kapur is shorter than I am, but much rounder. Except for the crinkles around his eyes, his face does not look old, but his hair is white, like his full beard.

"You must be tired after your long drive," I say to him. "Would you like some tea?"

He claps his hands together. "Perfect, thank you." He takes the glass and sips the tea.

"And you must be—" he says.

"Hastin," I say. "I am the elephant keeper."

"Hastin, would you like to work at my circus?" he asks.

I'm so surprised by his question, I wonder if I heard him right. With Timir standing so close, I am afraid to answer.

Ravi Kapur turns to Timir. "If that's all right with you, of course. Is the boy part of the deal, if I buy the elephant? I could use his experience."

I don't look at Timir, but I feel his glare and hear the tightening of his jaw when he answers. "Of course," he says.

"I could pay you eight rupees a day," Kapurji tells me.

"You mean you would pay me—actually hand me the money?" I put my hand in my pocket and hold on to Baba's stone.

By the way Sharad nudges my shoulder, I guess this is not the kind of thing a good businessman says.

Kapurji looks at Timir, then back at me. "Well, yes, if you are my employee, I will pay you money. Plus one trip home a year."

I wait for someone to start laughing, to tell me this is all a big joke.

No one laughs. I can hardly breathe.

"Don't you have a family you would like to visit now and then?" he asks.

"Yes," I manage to answer. "My mother"—my voice

catches in my throat—"and my sister." *Maybe, my sister,* I add silently. I imagine what Amma's face will look like when I hand her the money I have earned.

"If you prove to be a good worker, you can stay as long as you like."

That seems to mean I could also leave when I like, but I'm sure Sharad will nudge me very hard if I dare ask that right now.

"What kind of jobs do you have there?"

"My elephant keeper could use an assistant—you must know how much work they are. And you could help with our other animals. We have a hippo who never wants to wear her costume when it's showtime. Then there's a bear, a lion, monkeys—they are quite a handful, as you can imagine. Someone has to start and stop the music during the show. You must really pay attention to the performances to do that—the clowns, the acrobats, the animal acts. Or you could help serve food."

"You sell food there?"

"Oh yes, like samosas and sweets. We will keep you busy. There's always plenty to do at the circus."

A bus and taxi turn onto the road leading to the property.

Timir interrupts us. "I should show you to your seat. The performance will begin soon." Redness darkens his face.

"Yes, I'm excited to see what this elephant can do. We will talk more after the show, Hastin." He smiles.

Timir starts to lead him away, then turns to Sharad and mutters, "Don't let him too close to the elephant."

Ne Min sits on our wooden bench while we wait for the show to start, but I'm too nervous to sit down.

"Hastin, please," says Ne Min. "You're making me dizzy." I didn't realize until he mentioned it that I've been pacing in circles around the bench. I step to the fence and rest my arms on the top log, hands clasped as if I'm praying.

At last some dark clouds glide across the sky and cover the sun to give us a little relief from the heat.

Sharad and Nandita start the show with the hoop trick and I lean forward to watch them. *You'll get a barn, Nandita, a big barn,* I want to tell her. *And a real doctor to take care of you when you're sick.*

Somehow she seems to understand how important this show is. Nandita performs every trick just right. Even the new one—Sharad walks toward the audience as he speaks to them, and Nandita follows behind him on her hind legs. Her eyes look tired and she's a bit wobbly when she balances on the milk bottles, but people who don't know her may not notice.

A few raindrops hit my arms and head. Sometimes at home, after a long rain, I could smell the river in the red dirt walls of our hut. I swear I can smell my home right now.

Sharad and Nandita stand together in the arena, close to the audience. Finally, the last act is almost finished. I'm ready to leap over the fence and run to Nandita as soon as the show ends.

"Not a bad player for an elephant," Sharad says. He no longer calls her "a little elephant," since she is taller than he is. I laugh already, since I know what's about to happen. Then I stop.

"Why isn't she moving?" I say. Instead of stealing the ball from Sharad to make another goal, Nandita stands in place next to him. Sharad looks at her, then smiles nervously at the audience. He holds the ball more loosely in his hand, then bounces it on the ground right in front of Nandita, inviting her to steal it.

People shift in their seats and look at one another with questions on their faces. I scan the audience and recognize a few people who have attended the show before. They know what Nandita is supposed to do. I wish Sharad would end the show and tell everyone thank you and goodbye. Anything but this embarrassing silence. Nandita's trunk rests on the ground, and her body sways.

Ne Min stands up and steps to the fence.

The crowd gasps when Nandita staggers forward. She stares in my direction, but past me. Sharad steps toward Nandita as she sways, then he jumps aside as she crashes to the ground. A cloud of dust puffs up around her body.

Ne Min turns and shuffles toward the arena gate. As I climb onto the fence I glance at Kapurji. Timir grabs his arm while speaking frantically to him, but he breaks away and storms off.

I leap off the fence and run to Nandita, then fall to my knees and pet her trunk.

"Nandita, please be all right. You just have to be."

Her breathing is fast and raspy. Raindrops dot the dust on her skin.

The engine of Ravi Kapur's car roars.

Nandita does not look at me as I speak to her. Her eyes are closing, but the sliver I can still see is cloudy. I lean over and lay my cheek on her head, next to her ear.

"Please," I beg her. "Please stay with me."

Timir stands in the road and watches the car pull away. I imagine running past him, leaping onto the bumper of the car, and throwing myself onto the trunk, where I would ride all the way to the circus—my new boss, the animals, the music, samosas, money in my hand, a trip home . . .

Sharad is kneeling on the other side of Nandita, his hand on her back.

"A heatstroke. Go get some water," he tells me as Ne Min joins him at Nandita's side. "As much as you can carry. And some burlap bags. Hurry!"

I rush to the fence and scramble over it, then glance back at Nandita when my feet hit the ground on the other side. On my way to the water trough, I take just a moment to look behind me and watch everything I had hoped for drive away.

23

Elephants spend eighteen to twenty hours a day foraging for food.

—From *Care of Jungle Elephants* by Tin San Bo

My arms are shaking, but I don't know if it is from fear or work. Back and forth I have carried the metal bucket from the trough and poured water over Nandita's body.

A few people from the audience stand around the arena fence, watching. Others have left, holding the hands of their crying children. Some have entered the arena to help care for Nandita. From the supply shed I grabbed empty rice and flour bags, and we have soaked them in cold water to lay over Nandita's body. Timir paces alongside Nandita and yells at us, "Do something!" and "How could you let this happen?"

I want to run. I want to be far away from here, the gasping crowd, Timir, the heat. Nandita, the elephant I failed to protect. I have to get out of here. Now.

Slowly I back away from Nandita and look around. Everyone is focused on her. They won't notice if I slip away.

I hurry to the stable. What should I take with me? I grab the empty iodine bottle from under the straw and one of my Ganesh figures. The carvings of elephants I leave on the floor. As I glance around for anything else I might need, the palm leaf that Ne Min nailed to the wall catches my eye. *May those frightened cease to be afraid, and may those bound, be free.* I reach for it, then stop when I see Ne Min in the doorway.

"Do you think if you run away you will forget her?" He steps into the stable. "She is a part of you now, and you are a part of her. She will be with you always, no matter if you are here, or home, or the farthest place you could ever run."

Ne Min's dark brown eyes show the pain that they had when he first treated Nandita's hook wounds. "You have good memories of her now, but they will be forever shadowed by your abandonment. You are the one who cares for her most. You are the one she needs."

"Ne Min, I can't do this anymore. What use am I now? I've been her keeper all this time, and look at her. She is better off without me, and I don't want to be here when she—" I stop and turn away. "Please just let me go, and don't tell anyone I am leaving."

"No," he says. "Nandita still has a chance. I know what to do, but I cannot do it myself. If you leave now you are killing her, and you will not forgive yourself. Ever."

I gaze at the Ganesh carving in my hand, the first one I made here, that sits lopsided in the straw, that is still my favorite. *Remover of obstacles . . .*

My father used to tell me that sometimes we get help clearing obstacles from our path, and sometimes they are placed in our way. Later, when we are wiser and stronger, we may look back and feel thankful for what we had to overcome. Will I ever be thankful for anything that has happened to me? If only Baba had not died, and if Chanda had not been so sick, if we were not so poor . . .

I never would have met Nandita. How many people can say they have had an elephant for a best friend?

And I never would have met Ne Min. He stands next to me in the stable, quietly watching, knowing already what I will do, but knowing I have to decide for myself.

I set the Ganesh figure back in the corner of the stable. Underneath his right side I pile up some straw so he will not tip over.

"What do I need to do?"

"Nandita needs shade, but she will not be able to walk on her own yet. Gather some bamboo stalks and the biggest palm leaves you can. Help Sharad build a shelter over her."

"Will she be all right?" I remember asking Amma the same thing, the last time I saw Chanda.

"I don't know," says Ne Min. I hear an echo of Amma's voice adding, *"All we can do is pray."* And I will pray, but the not-knowing that gnaws at my stomach is the worst feeling of all.

After I talk to Sharad, I take the ax from the woodshed and hurry to a clump of bamboo. The stalks I chop have to be taller than Nandita. By the time I return to the arena with six long poles of bamboo, the audience members have left. Timir has retreated to his office. Ne Min sits next to Nandita with his hand on her forehead.

Sharad takes the bamboo from me, and I run to the palm trees. I swing the ax at the base of leaf after leaf, then fill my arms with as many as I can carry. Back in the arena, I place the leaves in a pile next to Nandita.

With a stick I dig a hole for the bamboo stalks, in four corners around Nandita's body. After Sharad places the end of each stalk into a hole, I fill in the dirt and pack it tightly. We will tie the two remaining stalks across the tops of the upright poles, so I grab the ladder from the supply shed. I hold each bamboo stalk in place as Sharad ties them with twine to the ones we placed in the ground.

"Now the roof," he says. "Chop some more stalks to lay across the top." I return to the trees and cut down an armful of bamboo. Sharad hands me the bamboo as I stand on the ladder so I can lay it across the poles to make the roof of the shelter. Maybe I'm seeing a bit of the goodness Ne Min was talking about that has been buried inside Sharad for so long.

While we work, I glance at Nandita to see if she looks any better. She is breathing easier, and her eyes are open but still cloudy. I pause in building the shelter to run to the spring for more water to keep her cool.

When bamboo stalks cross the top of the shelter from end to end, I cover them with palm leaves. Finally, Nandita is in the shade. From the stable I grab her wooden Ganesh and set it next to her so she can hold it in her trunk while she sleeps. Before I let go of it I say a silent prayer for her.

Ne Min tells me this will be Nandita's home for a few days, so I will need to haul some hay to the arena and bring her food and water. He has not asked me to sleep here with her but I will. If this is Nandita's home for now, it is also mine.

Sharad will lose two weeks' pay, and Timir added three months to my service. "Maybe you will remember to take better care of that animal," he'd said.

During the hottest part of the afternoon I pour water over Nandita's body. I keep a full bucket of water next to her, so when she is thirsty she only has to reach her trunk in and pour the water into her mouth. Much of the water spills on the ground while she lies on her side, but that evening she is able to hold her head up.

The next day, though, she doesn't seem to be any better.

Ne Min told me that a strong, healthy elephant would probably recover, but Nandita hasn't been healthy lately. If I were strong enough to carry her to the cool water of the spring, I would do it.

Even though I sleep outside with her now, I stop by the stable each night to carve a new mark on the wall. When will I get to go home? I imagine the marks stretching out in an endless row, to some faraway place that means never.

I bring Nandita mangoes and the pods from the tamarind tree, but she does not eat.

After my evening chores I go to the arena to check on her. I find Ne Min sitting next to her as he carves a block of wood. From my pocket I take a new elephant I have been working on and sit across from him.

"What are you making?" I ask. "I've never seen you carve before."

"I talked to Timir. When Nandita is strong enough, he will allow her to wander the grounds on her own more."

The thought of Timir listening to someone surprises me so much I can't speak. I wait for Ne Min to continue.

"Walking around to find some of her own food will be good for her. She knows what she should be eating, what she needs. If she eats better, her recovery will be quick. And the exercise will help. She will not move fast wearing shackles, but I told him I would make her a bell, so we can listen and find her if she wanders too far."

I take out my pocketknife and begin working on the

elephant figure as Ne Min smooths out his block of wood. When it is round like a tree branch, he whittles away at the center of it until it is hollowed out. He sets it on the ground like an upside-down cup, then carves a hole through it from one side to the other.

Next he carves two sticklike pieces with a hole through the top of each one. He threads a piece of thick twine through all three parts so that the sticks hang on either side of the cuplike piece. He closes his eyes and shakes the bell, listening to the *clip-clop-clip* sound the sticks make against the cup.

"Some elephants"—he laughs a little—"some of the smart ones, are mischievous." With the point of his knife he carves designs into the bell, and round letters like those on the palm leaf on my wall. "They clog their bell with mud to block its sound, if they wish to hide from you. Then you will have to search longer, but you will find her, and she will come to you."

As I listen to him, I carve behind one of the elephant's legs to make it look like it is bending a knee to step forward.

"You will become accustomed to the sound of her bell and be able to find her."

He stands up and ties the bell around Nandita's neck. I want to show him my elephant figure and ask if he thinks it is coming to life yet. But he walks away without saying good night.

• • •

Three days after Nandita's heatstroke, I return from the spring and laugh when I see her. She is standing next to what is left of the shelter, chewing on the bamboo poles. I wonder if when she woke up she thought a tree had grown right around her, like I used to think my home grew out of the ground.

Nandita's coarse red hair scratches my face when I hug her, but I don't care. "You had me so worried!" I tell her. For the first time since her collapse, I allow myself to cry.

She is wobbly on her feet, but I decide to take her to the spring. I lead her slowly out of the arena. The bell swings on Nandita's neck and makes its *clip-clop* sound as we walk.

Nandita almost runs the last few steps to the spring, then flops into the water. She rolls in the mud of the spring bed and sighs.

On the way back from the spring, I let her walk ahead of me to see where she will go. I follow her, and she finds a tree I've never seen before. The thick branches hang heavy with fruit the size of footballs. But it smells awful—like rotting onions—so I cannot believe Nandita would want to eat from this tree.

She wraps her trunk around a fruit and pulls it from a branch. It is so large, I'm not sure how she will eat it, but she places it whole into her mouth and bites down. As she chews I see the orange fruit inside her mouth, and its smell is sweeter. From a low branch I grab a fruit with both hands and pull. I place it on a flat stone and slice into it with my knife. The juice runs onto the green bumpy skin. The smell reminds me of bananas and something else—pineapple, maybe. I bite into it and realize that, again, Ne Min was right. Nandita knows where the good food is.

On the way back to the stable, Nandita follows me and taps my shoulder with her trunk like she did the night we tried to run away. I look around and pretend not to know who touched me. Nandita looks like she is laughing.

At lunch, I am so excited about Nandita's progress that I blurt out the good news to Ne Min without thinking. I should have waited until we were alone so Timir would not overhear me.

"All right then, she's better," says Timir. "We can start the show again soon."

"Not yet," warns Ne Min. "She is getting better, and she will live, but next time she may not be so lucky. It is too soon."

"Another week should be enough," Timir says, "She will be fine."

"You don't know that," says Ne Min. "She needs more rest, or she will be injured again, and what use will she be to you then?"

Sharad clears his throat. "Maybe he's right. Until we know it's safe for her to work—"

"That's enough!" Timir says. "I'm telling you, the

elephant will be fine. We have wasted too much time watching her sleep."

I clutch the stone in my pocket and finally speak up. "But you know Ne Min knows what he is talking about. He was right about—"

"I do not care to listen to the advice of an elephant killer," says Timir. "And neither should you."

No one says a word, no one moves, no one seems to breathe as we wait for what Ne Min will say. He must be furious. For Timir to suggest—

But Ne Min's face does not show anger, or denial, or even surprise. I am not sure what I'm seeing. He says nothing. Why won't he defend himself? His hands shake and he looks at the ground as he walks to the door. He glances up for just a moment as he passes me. Right before he looks away I see it.

Ne Min looks like Chanda did when she lied about taking two pieces of bread at dinner. He looks like Amma when she had to leave me at home alone to go work. So I recognize it, but still it does not make sense to me.

What I see in Ne Min's eyes is guilt.

24

Elephants communicate in ways we cannot hear.
　　—From *Care of Jungle Elephants* by Tin San Bo

The next night Nandita rolls in the dirt near the stable while I carve a new elephant out of mango wood.

I keep glancing toward the cook shed, waiting for Ne Min to walk out. There must be some explanation for Timir calling him an elephant killer, but I cannot imagine what it is. Ne Min would never harm an elephant.

After breakfast I started to bring it up, but he interrupted. "How is Nandita? Should I check on her?"

"No," I answered too quickly. He looked as if I'd slapped him. "I mean—she is doing much better, but of course you can check on her anytime."

He picked up a broom and started sweeping the floor. "We need more firewood, Hastin." I left the cook shed to collect more wood, even though a small pile was already stacked next to the stove.

I want to show him my new carvings. I'm sure he will like them. They look more like real animals now. I might be good enough to sell my wood carvings one day, like my father did. Perhaps I could even set up a table in the marketplace. I think of the wood-carver I met there and the elephant box he made with all the tiny elephants inside. A good gift for Chanda, I thought at the time.

Suddenly Nandita stops rolling in the dirt and stands up. She stares into the distance, perfectly still, her ears flat against her head, her trunk in the air. I stand next to her to see what caught her attention, but I don't notice anything.

Then the hairs on my arms and the back of my neck stand straight up. It takes my brain a moment to catch up to what my body already senses. Timir is behind us. At the last *click* of his cane I turn to face him. I still hold the carving in my hand. There is no time to hide it. He'll know now that I have a knife. Certainly he won't allow me to keep it. What will I do without Baba's knife?

He looks down at me and holds out his hand. I place the mango wood elephant in his palm. He seems to stare right through me, as if he can see exactly what I have been thinking.

He looks at the elephant from all sides. "You hardly have time for a hobby," he says. "But maybe we could sell something like this at the show. People may like a souvenir to take home." He tosses the figure back to me. "Make some more of these before the next show. Perhaps you can earn a little extra money for your family."

He turns to walk away. "But first"—he stops and looks back at me—"go to the cook shed and see that everything is put away. That cook had to go home early."

In the days before the next show, I spend as much time carving as I can. I make elephants of all sizes, and a few Ganesh figures. I work late into the night, wondering how much the carvings will sell for and what my family will buy with the money. Some food, of course, and maybe enough cloth for Amma to make new saris for herself and Chanda. I also start making an elephant box for Chanda that I will fill with small wooden elephants. This I hide in a corner of the stable, under the straw, to take with me when I leave.

I keep interrupting my work to check on Nandita. She looks healthy—her eyes are bright and clear, and she eats more than ever. When she forages in the woods, I can hardly keep up with her despite her shackles. Luckily the *clip-clop* of the wooden bell leads me to her when she wanders too far ahead of me. Sometimes when she approaches me from behind, I pretend not to hear the bell or the rustling grass under her footsteps. Nandita likes to sneak up on me and tap my shoulder with her trunk. Then when I turn around she looks like she's laughing.

We have a full crowd for Nandita's first show after her illness. I grip the edge of the fence during the entire performance and have to keep reminding myself to breathe. Nandita kicks the last goal in the game and runs circles around Sharad, who throws down his hat and pretends to be angry. The performance is perfect.

Timir set up a table near the audience to display my wood carvings. He works behind the table, where he places the money from customers in a metal box. From the arena, where I clean up after the show, I overhear some of the buyers.

"What beautiful carvings!"

"Such detail!"

"You are a skilled wood-carver," one man says to Timir. He buys a whole family of wooden elephants.

I imagine selling my carvings in the marketplace, just like Baba did, and bringing home presents for my family with the money I earn.

"Thank you, I do my best," Timir answers.

I stop working and hold my pitchfork still to listen closer.

"Really, you are too modest," says the customer. "An artisan like yourself could make a good living selling these carvings in town. You could open your own shop.

Of course we love the elephant show, so we hope you'll do no such thing."

Timir glances at me, then looks back to the buyer. "Yes, thank you. Hope to see you again."

When the last customer leaves, the table is bare. Every one of my carvings has sold. Timir picks up the money box. He does not look at me as he heads to his office.

I throw the pitchfork aside and storm to Timir's office. He is so busy counting money he doesn't notice me standing in the doorway. My hand in my pocket clutches the stone.

My throat tightens up like it will not let me speak. Timir jumps when I clear it and ask, "How much money did I earn for my family?"

"What? Oh yes, your family. Well, of course you do have to pay me back for providing your room here all this time . . ."

"My room? But that was part of our agreement! And I live in a stable!"

Timir's face hardens. "And the wood for those carvings. Since I own this land, I own the trees on it, too. I will take what is mine, and if there's anything left, I'll send it to your family. Who knows? They might be able to move into a bigger shack, one without a dirt floor."

That night I pace back and forth in the stable, too angry to sleep. I pound the wall so hard that pieces of bark fall onto the ground below. I don't notice until I slump onto the floor, arm muscles burning, how badly the rough logs scraped my hands.

Nandita stands and moves closer to lie down next to me. She seems to know when I'm feeling bad. It's like Ne Min said: she doesn't understand the words, but she understands me.

I lean against her and stare through the spaces between the stable logs. Tonight's moon, bright and mango orange, hangs low in the sky, just above the treetops. If I followed it, it would guide me home. But I am trapped here, like one of Timir's animals who once lived in the now-rusty cages.

Instead of climbing into my hammock, I decide to sleep here with Nandita like I used to. I don't mind the small space I have to sleep in. Next to Nandita I almost feel at home.

In the morning I wake early and take the elephant box for Chanda from underneath the straw. I will not carve for Timir anymore, since he will take everything I earn for himself. From now on every wood carving I make will be for my family.

I carve two more elephants on one side of the box, so now a full line of elephants marches trunk to tail around all four sides. The box is filled with the small elephants I have carved. Some are the size of my smallest fingernail like the wooden elephants in the box from the marketplace in the city, but others are as big as my thumb. Their colors are different, too—most are the gray of mango wood or the light brown of the sal tree. The heart of the tamarind tree is strong, its wood hard to carve, but I used it for a few elephants because Chanda will like its color of deep purplish brown. The thought jumps into my mind that she may not be at home to take my gift, but I push it away and keep carving.

I'm at the woodpile, almost finished with my morning chores, when I realize something is wrong. Mid-chop, I drop the ax. No smoke pours from the cook shed's chimney. Usually Ne Min is here by now. I run to the cook shed and call his name.

The cook shed is empty. I run a circle around the outside of the building.

"Ne Min?" I call again.

Only the morning birds answer me.

25

The tamest elephant is still a wild animal.
—From *Care of Jungle Elephants* by Tin San Bo

I stand on the path that leads to Ne Min's home. I've never seen where he lives, only the path he takes. But he might walk far, or turn down other trails along the way, so I do not know where to look for him.

He's probably just running late. If Timir shows up and breakfast is not ready, he will be furious with Ne Min. But I don't dare leave to go look for him. Timir might think I ran away, and he won't wait for an explanation before hitting me with his cane.

Back in the cook shed I take a metal bowl from a shelf and set it on the counter. A cool pot of water waits on the stove where I placed it earlier, and I light the fire beneath it now.

I've never made breakfast by myself before, but I think I've helped Ne Min enough to figure it out. I step outside but still don't see him.

Nandita trumpets at me from the stable as I run to the trees to collect mangoes. I pick more than we need for the meal, since Nandita will complain if I do not offer some to her.

On my way back she is reaching her trunk through the logs of the stable. I open the door and hand a fruit to her. While she places it in her mouth, I set another mango on the ground next to her before I return to the cook shed. I leave the door open so she can walk around on her own to look for more food if she wants to.

As I peel the mangoes I peek outside now and then, hoping to see Ne Min shuffling up the path. Finally I spot him, after I chop the last of the fruit. My relief mixes with worry when I see that he is moving slower than usual. I set the knife down and run to meet him.

"I am fine, Hastin," he says before I can ask. "Hard to sleep last night." Again he assures me that he is all right, but I take his arm anyway and walk to the cook shed with him.

We work together to make breakfast. Ne Min mixes the dough, and I break it into small pieces to roll between my palms. With his rolling pin he flattens each piece into a paper-thin circle. We deep-fry the dough, and it swells in the hot oil. I stir the mangoes in a pot on the stove while Ne Min seasons them.

Breakfast is ready just before Timir and Sharad arrive. The roti is almost too hot to eat. Steam rises from its soft center when I bite into it. The mangoes are perfectly sweet and spicy and salty. When I get up to fill my plate again, Ne Min asks for another helping, too.

One evening Nandita rolls in the dust while I clean the arena. Everyone else has left for the day, and I am ready to finish my work and head to my hammock. I've kept making the marks on the stable, even after they let me know I'm supposed to be home.

Nandita stands and circles her trunk in the dirt, collects a pile of dust, and throws it over her back. She tosses some dirt in my direction.

"Nandita, stop that!" I laugh as I shake the dirt out of my hair. She looks like she is laughing, too.

Then she freezes. She raises her trunk high and flattens her ears against her head as she stares at the distant trees.

"What is it, Nandita?" As I step closer I notice the air trembles as if shaken by thunder, but the sky is clear and quiet.

I hold my hand up to pet Nandita, and vibrations tickle my palm. She doesn't move when I rest my hand high on her trunk, then her forehead. Here is where the silent rumbling comes from. My hand and arm tingle all the way to my shoulder. I follow her gaze, toward the trees. For the longest time we stand there together, my hand on her forehead.

Finally I hear it—the calls of the wild elephants. I have heard them before, but this time they do not sound so far away. The tops of the trees shake, and Nandita and I watch, still and silent.

The elephants emerge from the trees, looking larger and larger as they head closer to the place that has been our home for so long.

As they approach I look at each elephant, one by one. Some are Nandita's size. Some look older, like the bull that Ne Min and I saw—tall and heavy, with tattered ears and splotches on the face and trunk where gray skin has faded to pink. One of the youngest is just starting to grow his tusks. Unlike the bull's, they are bright white, smooth and unbroken. My eyes stop scanning the herd when I notice who is behind him. The elephant who nudges him to keep up with the herd has skin like moonlight through a storm cloud.

Indurekha. Moonbeam.

At times I have wondered about her, but I always picture her as the young elephant I first saw in the forest, wrestling with Nandita in the river.

The elephants stop walking when they reach the fence surrounding the property. My hand slides off Nandita's head as she leaves my side. I open the arena gate to allow her to approach the herd.

Their excitement turns into a storm of thundering blasts, flapping ears, swaying trunks, and spinning. Some of the older ones reach over the wires of the fence to touch Nandita's head and face, and they put their trunks into one another's mouths. Indurekha pushes her way to the front of the crowd, and she and Nandita entwine their trunks. A large elephant rumbles and plows through the herd to reach the fence. She looks like Sanjana, the one whose trumpet of rage at the trap told me that she was Nandita's mother. Indurekha steps aside. Sanjana touches Nandita's face with her trunk.

After some time the storm quiets. Nandita is with her herd but not truly with them. They will move on, while she stands behind the fence that imprisons her.

The largest elephant is the first to walk away, followed by the smallest. One by one the elephants step away, some of them reaching out their trunks again to touch Nandita's face.

Sanjana alone remains by the fence. She wraps her trunk around Nandita's, and the two of them talk in low grumbles. They separate, and Nandita's mother gazes at the departing herd before she, too, turns to leave.

Nandita calls out and walks alongside her as far as the fence will allow, then watches as her family leaves her for the second time in her life.

Nandita has grown so much she won't fit through the

wooden gate anymore, so I run to the large metal gate, hoping that it isn't locked. As always, though, it's held closed with a padlock and a rusty chain wrapped around the fence post.

I hurry to the woodshed. *Where is the ax?* I kick the woodpile and toss aside logs. Quickly I search the area and see the ax handle sticking out from under a log.

Nandita has not moved from the spot where she watches the herd. I run to the fence.

I raise the ax high and chop at the fence post next to the gate. Wood chips fly away as I chop again and again. If I keep working, I know I can break through it to release the gate. Though my arms feel weak and tired, I hack at the fence some more.

Nandita watches me as I work. I think I'm getting close to breaking through the post. A few more chops should do it. I rest my hands on my knees and turn toward the forest. I can still see the elephant herd, but they grow smaller and smaller.

Again I raise the ax for another chop, then stop when I notice the chain. Not the one at the gate's handle, but the one that shackles Nandita's front legs. I drop the ax and slump to the ground.

Even if Nandita can get away from here, she cannot run free. She won't be able to keep up with a herd in the wild, and what about when she grows? With no one to unlock the shackles and loosen them, they will cut into her legs as the years pass.

Then I think of my pocketknife. It has served me well for carvings, but I wonder if I could use it to pick the lock on the shackles. It wouldn't be easy, but with time I think I could do it. I will let her out of the gate, then grab my bag and catch up with her to unlock her shackles.

Next to me, Nandita sways back and forth. This is her best chance to run away from here, and I cannot let it pass by. I stand and pick up the ax. Once again I raise it. This time something else stops me.

Sharad's truck sputters to a halt at the fence behind the cook shed. What is he doing here?

Pieces of the fence post are chopped away, but the chain still holds the gate closed. And I am out of time.

"Go on, old friend," I urge Nandita. "Look at what a strong elephant you are now." I grab the fence and shake it, and push it open as far as the chain will allow. Nandita steps closer, and I pull the gate toward us, then push it back. When I pull the gate again, she places her forehead against it and pushes.

"Good girl, Nandita," I say as I reach up to hug her. "Keep doing that, and you will have the forest again. Nothing is holding you here anymore."

I look behind me at the empty cook shed. I wish Ne Min were here so I could tell him goodbye. It would be hard, though, and I wouldn't know how to tell him how thankful I am for everything he has done for me. Maybe it is better this way. But if he were here, I think I know what he would say: *Nothing holds you here either. Go.*

While Nandita pushes at the gate, I run to the stable. From underneath the straw I grab my Ganesh figure and Nandita's, Chanda's elephant box, and the bag Ne Min gave me, which still holds the iodine bottle. Last I remove Ne Min's leaf from its nail on the stable wall. I stuff the carvings and the leaf into my bag as I hurry out of the stable.

On my way back to the fence, I see Sharad. Nandita still pushes on the gate with her head.

"Stop!" Sharad yells as he runs to her. In his right hand he holds the elephant hook. I drop my bag and run toward Nandita, but Sharad is much closer.

"Stop!" he shouts again. At the sound of his voice, Nandita turns to him. Sharad raises the hook. Nandita raises her trunk. The slap when she hits him is louder than the sound of his body crashing against the fence.

Sharad lies on the ground, not moving.

26

An elephant's memory is longer than life and stronger than death.

   —From *Care of Jungle Elephants* by Tin San Bo

Nandita trumpets and runs around, stepping close to Sharad's body.

"Nandita, stop!" I yell. She nudges Sharad with her trunk. I walk up to her and place my hand on her forehead. She spins away from me with a roar, her trunk flailing. I grab on to the swinging chain around her neck and am able to calm her enough to guide her to the arena.

I run back to the fence to check on Sharad. His chest moves up and down as he breathes, but he still does not seem to be awake. I pace back and forth as I try to figure out what to do.

There is no way I can carry Sharad or even drag him

indoors. From the stable I grab my blanket, then lay it flat on the ground next to him. With both hands I roll him onto the blanket. I look from the bleeding wound on Sharad's forehead to Nandita. Should I help him now or work on the gate to set us free?

Maybe this is one of those times Baba talked about, when Ganesh puts obstacles in our way.

I take Baba's stone from my pocket while I think. Ne Min told me there is goodness in Sharad, however buried it is.

I have a family to take care of. I remember Sharad telling me.

I turn the stone over in my palm. I wish there were a way to save the good Sharad and leave the mean Sharad on the ground. But I can't do that any more than I could throw aside the dark layers of my stone while hanging on to the light. If I run away from the Sharad who hurts Nandita, I also abandon the one who built a shelter for her, and the one who is the father of five children.

From the supply shed I grab a bottle of iodine and some cloth bandages, then run to the cook shed for a bowl. I hurry to the trough and scoop the bowl into the water before returning to Sharad's side.

Nandita rocks herself back and forth in the arena. Her chain rattles as she bangs it against a fence post. I look toward the forest, to where the elephants have disappeared. Nandita wants to be with her family as much as I do. And they want her back, too.

"Sharad?" I kneel next to him and nudge his shoulder. He does not wake up. I wonder if Nandita will be punished for hurting him. Maybe Sharad will be thankful I helped him when he was hurt and won't want her to get in trouble.

I pour a little of the water onto Sharad's forehead, then blot the wound clean with a cloth. I turn the cloth over and soak it with iodine, then dab his head.

A spot of blood seeps through his pants near the knee. When I roll up the leg of his pants I see a small, round sore on his outer thigh. It looks just like a hook wound. The elephant hook rests in the dirt near the fence. He must have gouged himself when Nandita knocked him aside. I pour iodine on a new cloth and clean the wound again. Sharad moves his head to the side and groans.

Perhaps I am foolish for not running while I have the chance, but when I think of leaving right now, my stomach tightens like I'm doing something wrong. I can escape with Nandita later, after I know Sharad will be all right.

Sharad stirs and groans. His eyes flicker open.

"Sharad? I need to get you some help. Do you know where Ne Min lives?"

"I'll be fine," he says. He starts to sit up, then groans again and holds his head. After he lies back down, he points toward the cook shed. "You know the trail back there?"

"Yes, I know where to start," I say.

"Follow it until it divides. The trail to the left leads to a small shack."

"Can you hold this in place?" I lay Sharad's hand on the bandage that covers his head wound. "Press down to slow the bleeding," I say before I hurry to the wooden gate behind the cook shed and down the trail that leads to Ne Min's home.

After I run for some time, I start to wonder if I could have passed the turn. I stop and look behind me and wish I'd picked up a lantern from the cook shed. The thickness of the trees here blocks out the last light of the evening. It would be easy to miss a break in the trail. But when I run a little farther I see the divided path ahead of me.

Down the trail to the left I run, then stop when I hear Nandita's bell. But I chained her up in the arena—how could she be here? I look around and listen. Nandita is nowhere in sight. The bell rings again, and I realize I was wrong. It is not the same sound as Nandita's bell—close, but it rings with a higher tone. I continue down the path.

There it is—a small wooden shack among the trees. The wind blows, and I hear the bell again. On the tree in front of me, next to the window of the home, a wooden bell hangs from a branch. When I get closer I see it is much like Nandita's, but parts of it are black like coal and it is not as smooth. It looks like something I could have carved a few months ago.

I knock on the shack's flimsy door and call to Ne Min. When he doesn't answer I open the door.

I step into the only room of Ne Min's home. An old wooden chair sits in one corner, and against the opposite wall is his cot, where he is sleeping right now. On a table next to his bed, I recognize the book I have seen him read, with pictures of elephants and handwriting of loops and circles.

I sit on the edge of Ne Min's cot and light the lamp on the table.

"Ne Min?" I say as I gently shake his shoulder.

He does not wake up, so I try again. "Ne Min, please, it's important."

Ne Min wakes with a jolt, as if I've poured a tub of cold water on him.

"I'm sorry to wake you," I tell him, "but Sharad is hurt. Can you come help?"

Ne Min sits up and looks around, then rubs his eyes. He takes my hand so I can help him up. As we walk out the door I tell him about Nandita hitting Sharad.

On the path that leads back to the circus grounds, Ne Min tells me to go ahead of him and sit with Sharad. He will catch up to me there.

By the time I return to Sharad the bandage on his head is soaked with blood. He looks away from me, then winces and squeezes his eyes shut when I press a clean bandage over the old one. We say nothing to each other while we wait for Ne Min.

When Ne Min arrives, he checks Sharad's head wound and cleans it with more iodine. Sharad winces and tries to knock Ne Min's hand away.

"Stop—that stings!" he says. "You're hurting me worse than the elephant did."

Ne Min stays calm and ignores the batting of Sharad's hands. "We must keep the wound clean," he says.

"It's clean enough!" He starts to sit up, then curses and grabs his side that Nandita hit with her trunk.

As Ne Min cleans and wraps the hook wound on Sharad's leg, I swear I see him smile just a little.

"We should take you indoors," says Ne Min. "Do you think you can stand, if we help you?"

Sharad sits up, then groans and holds his head.

"Slowly," says Ne Min. "Do not try to get up too fast."

Sharad hangs on to the fence with one hand and clutches his side with the other. Ne Min and I stand next to him to support him. He leans on the fence for a while after standing, then we each hold on to an arm to lead him to Timir's office.

"Just wait until Timir hears about this," Sharad says as we pass the arena. He nods toward Nandita, then turns to Ne Min. "You have a good recipe for elephant stew?" He laughs hard, then winces in pain.

Ne Min and I glance at each other across the doubled-over Sharad. I'm not sure what Ne Min is thinking, but I know I'd like to throw Sharad back to Nandita.

"Hastin, we should clean Sharad's wounds again. Will

you get the iodine bottle?" Ne Min smiles at me as we lay Sharad on the sofa in Timir's office.

It is not until I am almost asleep in my hammock that night that I realize I had not asked Ne Min about the wooden bell that hangs outside his window.

After I feed Nandita in the morning I decide to keep her in the stable so Timir won't see her when he arrives. Ne Min must be tired from having his sleep interrupted. It's time to make breakfast, but again the cook shed is empty. While the water heats on the stove, I go to Timir's office to check on Sharad.

Before I reach the office I hear his snoring. The bandage around his head slipped a little during the night. He does not stir from his sleep when I adjust it to cover his injury. I wonder what Timir's reaction will be when he finds out what happened.

On my way out of the office, I stop in the doorway and turn around. My eyes go right to his front pocket—the pocket where he keeps his ring of keys. One of those keys would unlock the metal gate, and another would release Nandita's shackles. I feel so stupid for not thinking of this last night, but in all the commotion it didn't occur to me.

Without making a sound I step back to the sofa. I crouch down and move aside the blanket, then pause. Sharad's snoring continues, so I slip my hand into his front pocket.

Nothing. I reach over to the other side and pat the left pocket, hoping to hear a jingle of keys. Still nothing.

Where could he have put them? I scan the floor around the couch, then return to the doorway and look toward the arena. Think. When we were helping him last night, I don't remember hearing the keys or seeing the bulk of the key ring in his pocket. Maybe I just didn't notice them, but maybe he left them somewhere else.

Outside, I wander behind the office while I think. I still don't know why Sharad came back last night, but I remember hoping he was stopping by for a short time before leaving again.

So if it was a quick stop . . .

I run to the wooden gate behind the cook shed and throw it open, then hurry to Sharad's truck. As soon as I open the passenger-side door I see it dangling from the ignition—Sharad's key ring. Already I feel closer to home.

Timir will be here soon, and we don't have time to get far enough away to escape. I'll leave with Nandita early tomorrow morning, long before he arrives. After slipping the key ring into my pocket I push the truck door closed with a quiet *click*.

On my way to the woodshed, the damaged fence post catches my eye. I haven't thought about how to explain why pieces of it are chopped away. I still wonder if I did the right thing last night. One moment I know I did, and the next moment I want to bang my head on the fence for not escaping when I had the chance.

Then I remember the hook. It must still be there on the ground where Sharad dropped it. The keys jingle in my pocket as I run to the gate. There, lying in the dirt, is the hook. My hand shakes as I reach for it. The icy metal chills my palm when I grasp the handle. It is the first time I have ever held it.

And it will be the last time anyone ever holds it. I hurry through the trees, not stopping until I reach the spring.

With all my strength I throw the hook that has caused Nandita so much pain. It splashes into the water, where I hope it will lie there and turn to rust.

I have chopped all the fruit for breakfast, and Ne Min still isn't here. The mangoes cook in a pot over the fire, and I pick up the spice jars one by one. So many of them look the same to me. Ne Min enters the cook shed as I'm trying to figure out which spices to use. He looks like he could use a few more hours of sleep.

"Thank you for starting breakfast again, Hastin. I am sorry I am late."

"I don't mind, Ne Min. You needed the rest. If you would like to sleep more, I could—"

He takes the jar I am holding and smiles. "Looks like I arrived just in time to save breakfast. Not good with fruit, this one." He sets the jar on the counter and picks up two others. "But I trust you with the sugar. Pour a handful into the pot."

We both turn quiet when we hear the approach of

Timir's truck. It might be better to tell him myself what happened, but I cannot move. He'll have to discover for himself that Sharad is sleeping in his office with a bandaged head.

Ne Min touches my shoulder, then grabs two spice jars in one hand.

"These," he says, "good for fruit." He sets them down and picks up a jar filled with tiny black seeds. "Best for seasoning vegetables." Next he points to a dark brown spice. "That one will set your tongue on fire, so use only a little."

We continue cooking in silence. I suspect that like me, Ne Min is trying to understand the shouted words from Timir's office.

Breakfast waits on the table, and Ne Min and I sit down to eat by ourselves. I wish I could enjoy the peaceful meal but I'm too nervous. My stomach bunches into a knot when I hear the *click-step* of Timir's approach. He stomps into the cook shed. His cane slaps the table. If I look up I imagine I will see his face redder than ever and about to explode.

"I remember when we first caught that elephant," he says. "Sharad warned me that she had a temper. It seems he was right. Now we have to start again with a new one, after we dispose of that failure. And you"—he slides his cane back, then presses the end of it to my chest—"you will stay here and continue to be the elephant caretaker. I expect you to do a better job controlling the next one.

I cannot have my trainer getting killed because of your incompetence." He shoves me with his cane and turns to leave.

"But, Timir," I say, "it was not the elephant's fault. She—"

He stops and turns to me. "Yes, you are right. It's your fault, so consider yourself her murderer."

"That's enough!" snaps Ne Min. He rushes toward Timir. "He did nothing wrong—"

Without taking his eyes off me, Timir reaches out and shoves Ne Min aside. Ne Min's body slams against the stove. He slumps to the floor, clutching his side.

"Ne Min!" I jump up from the table and run to him.

"Oh, one more thing." Timir speaks as if nothing has happened, like my first day here when he killed the mouse with his cane. "The keys."

I ignore him. "Ne Min, are you all right? Don't try to stand yet."

Timir smacks me in the head with his cane. "The keys!"

I look up at him. "What?"

"Sharad's key ring is missing. He said it was in his truck, but it's gone. Give it to me."

This is what he cares about now, when Ne Min so obviously needs help.

Timir swings his cane toward me again. Before it hits me, I grab it. I stand up and hold each end, then raise my knee to snap the cane in two against my leg.

I fling aside the broken pieces of cane, then take the

keys from my pocket. With all the anger and all the hate I feel for Timir, I throw the key ring across the room. It clatters against the wall and drops to the floor. I'm glad Amma is not around to hear what I call Timir.

"I'm going to town to hire some new workmen—and someone who owns an elephant gun," he says. "When I come back tomorrow, you will help them dig a trap." He picks up the keys and walks out.

I kneel next to Ne Min. "Let me see your side."

He moves his hand away so I can lift his shirt to see where he hit the stove. Already some of the skin is turning purple. He winces when I touch the area. Hopefully he didn't break a rib.

"You should go home and lie down," I say. "Can you stand if I help you?"

"Yes, I think so," he says. He grabs on to the stove with one hand while I support his other side, then I walk him to his house.

That evening Sharad insists he is ready to go home, but I wish he would stay one more night. He sleeps so soundly, I think I could sneak into the office and take the keys again. Somehow I must get Nandita out of here before Timir returns tomorrow.

"Looks like I won't have much work here for a while," Sharad says when I take a plate of dinner to him, "until we have a new elephant to train. But I'll come back tomorrow to help with the new trap."

I remember the ax. Since I cannot get the keys back, I will try again to chop away at the fence post. But before Sharad goes to his truck, he limps to the woodshed to retrieve the ax. I know I will not be left alone with it again.

While cleaning up after dinner I think about what to do about Nandita. I must find a way to let her go, but I don't see how it is possible. Maybe Ne Min will have an idea.

Ne Min is sound asleep on his cot. I light the lamp and see that some of the color has returned to his face. When he wakes up for a moment I offer to stay.

"Of course not," he says. "Where would you sleep?"

"The chair," I answer, "or the floor. I don't mind."

"It is late. Go back to Nandita and your hammock," he says. "I will see you in the morning."

I do lie in my hammock that night, but I do not sleep.

While breakfast simmers on the stove I decide to visit Ne Min again. Sharad parks his truck just as I am leaving the cook shed.

"Where are you going?" he asks me.

"To check on Ne Min."

"Never mind that, I'll go. You get breakfast ready."

"But—" I want to go myself, and talk to Ne Min about Nandita.

Sharad starts down the path to Ne Min's house.

I wish I could grab both Nandita and Ne Min and run

away from here and keep running until I was home with Amma and Chanda.

When Sharad returns to the cook shed, he is out of breath and clutching his side.

"I'll finish up here," he says. Sharad has never offered to work in the cook shed before. "Quickly, before Timir gets here," he says when I don't move. "Ne Min wants to see you."

27

You cannot leave the elephants behind, no matter how far you go. You are a part of them and they are a part of you. Keep this book to help you care for them, for one day they will return to you.

—Written on the inside front cover of *Care of Jungle Elephants* by Tin San Bo to his son, Ne Min

The trees around me are a blur as I race to Ne Min's house. Without knocking I run inside and sit on the edge of the cot. Ne Min looks like he is sleeping. I take his hand in mine. His other hand clutches something that looks like a square of paper. By its worn edge, I slip it out of his hand.

The photograph is faded with age, but I recognize the face that looks out at me as a much younger Ne Min. He stands next to an elephant. One hand is on her trunk, as if he'd been petting her before he turned to the camera. What I notice most about the picture is that Ne Min looks happy. This picture was taken before his eyes were sad.

When Ne Min finally speaks, he does not open his eyes.

"I thought I heard her," he says. "The bell."

"No, I came by myself. Nandita's in the stable," I say.

"No, not her. Another one."

He quiets again. It seems like he is still sleeping. Maybe he does not even realize he spoke.

"Her name was Myit Ko Naing. She saved my life." Ne Min opens his eyes and looks right at me. "You want to know why I know so much and say so little. She meant the world to me but I could not save her."

I want to ask him who he is talking about, but I wait for him.

"We were born on the same night. An elephant cow that belonged to my family gave birth to her calf while my mother gave birth to me. The calf was a good elephant, and often walked by my side." Ne Min stops and takes a deep, raspy breath.

"If someone new approached, she would flare out her ears and step in front of me. When we were young she was called Khin Ma Ye—'She Who Is Friendly and Brave.' The connection we shared was strong, like the bond that ties you to Nandita.

"When I was three years old, I wandered too close to the river that ran through the teak forest where we lived.

I fell in, and villagers ran to the river when they heard my screams. On the riverbank, they tried to outrun the water that carried me away. But the rains that year were plenty, so the river was high and the current strong."

Ne Min stops to catch his breath, as if telling the story wears him out.

"Then, higher on the bank," he continues, "Khin Ma Ye ran past everyone and into the river ahead of me. Like a huge boulder she stood, then reached out her trunk and grabbed me when I floated by. She lifted me out of the water and placed me safely on the riverbank. That night my father chose her new name, Myit Ko Naing."

"Why?" I stop to clear my throat so I can speak in more than a whisper. "What does that mean?"

"It means 'The One Who Conquered the River.'"

Ne Min is quiet for so long I think he must have fallen asleep again. When he coughs, I set the picture aside and help him sit up—just a little because it hurts his side. I give him a drink of water from a metal cup on his bedside table. He lies back down and takes time to catch his breath again.

"When I was ten years old I carved her a bell. She liked to wander, but I always found her. Soon I learned to find her bell among all the others. Our village had many elephants, but the noise of the bells I did not carve sounded too high, or too low, or too hollow."

He reaches for his cup again. With one hand I lift his head while I give him a sip of water.

"One summer evening many years later, I sat outside my tent by torchlight to carve a new bell for a young elephant. I remember a cool gust of wind, and I hoped it would bring rain, for the river was low and the trees dry.

"I do not remember falling asleep, but I woke to the smell of smoke and the heat of flames. My knife and wood block had fallen to the ground. So had my torch."

Ne Min takes a few wheezing breaths.

"From one tent to another I ran, to warn everyone of the fire. As we escaped from the forest, I listened for the bell of Myit Ko Naing, but I heard nothing over the crackling of flames and the snapping of tree limbs. Other animals ran away from the fire, so I decided she must be safe somewhere, and we would find each other soon. But the fire moved on and the panic died down, and still I did not see my elephant."

As Ne Min rests, I listen to the wooden bell that swings on the branch outside his window.

"I hurried back into the village," he says. "Near the place my hut had been, I found her. Why would she be there? What kind of animal runs into a fire? Maybe the black smoke that had surrounded us confused her, and she had not known which way to run. Or is it possible she was looking for me?

"I ran to her and called her name. I fell to my knees and placed my hand on her side. She was still breathing."

Ne Min pauses again, then speaks louder than I have ever heard him speak.

" '*Tah!* Stand up!' I ordered her. She opened one eye and looked up at me, as if to say she was sorry she could not obey my command. She moved her trunk, just a little, and touched my hand. Then she was gone.

"In the days after she died, I found myself listening for her bell. But only the notes that were too high, or too low, or too hollow filled the air. When I first awoke in the mornings I would set out to look for her, wondering if she was eating bamboo or if I would find her in a patch of tall kaing grass near the river. Then the remembering would hit me with a pain that dropped me to the ground."

Ne Min breaks from his storytelling to rest, and his breathing is shallow and crackly.

Suddenly everything makes sense to me. How he seems to know all there is to know about elephants, always knows how to help Nandita, and shows such pain when she is hurt. And of course he never wanted to talk about why, and at times was too hurt by his memories to even go near Nandita. Just then I remember Timir's comments about Ne Min being an "elephant killer."

"You told Timir about this?" I ask.

"A long time ago. He wanted to know why I left home, and I told him the whole story—my fallen torch, the fire, the pain and guilt I have lived with every day since I lost her."

And Timir used Ne Min's guilt to make him feel even worse.

"When I told my family I was leaving," Ne Min

continues, his voice shaky, "they tried to talk me out of it. That's who we were, that's what we always did—we took care of the elephants who hauled timber. I didn't know any other life. But no one understood. Her silence made everything else too loud."

He speaks so quietly now, I have to lean closer to hear him.

"You were not born among elephants, but somehow you have a heart for them, like I do. And Nandita has a heart for you. She would lay down her life for you, like Myit Ko Naing did for me. You must do all you can now to save her. And yourself."

"But, Ne Min, I don't know how. I can't get the ax, or the keys . . ."

He squeezes my hand. "If you do not want to carry her death on your shoulders for the rest of your life, you will not let anything stop you."

I used to think the guilt I'd seen on Ne Min's face was about Anju, from Timir's old circus, since he couldn't talk Timir out of killing her. He must have felt so much worse about Myit Ko Naing, having grown up with her and knowing she died in the fire he caused.

His hand starts to slip away from mine. I grip it tighter.

"Ne Min, wait—" There are so many more questions I have for him, so much more I want to say to him, so much to thank him for.

"No, Hastin," he says. "Remember the candles? It is

time for my flame to die out now. What keeps me alive will breathe life into something new."

I cling to Ne Min to keep him from slipping away. He can't leave. I don't care about the something new out there—I need the old Ne Min here. I lay my head on his shoulder and drape my arm across his chest like I'm shielding a candle flame from the wind. My arm moves up and down with Ne Min's breathing, then grows still.

The light that is Ne Min's life fades away, and moves on to give life to someone else, somewhere else. All that's left here is sadness, and it fills the room.

Outside, the wind blows, and rings the wooden bell with a sound that is not too high, or too low, or too hollow.

28

A young elephant that is chained will try hard to free itself, but once it gives up, it gives up forever. Even when it is strong enough to break its chains, it will not. So it is that the smallest chain can hold the largest elephant.
—From *Care of Jungle Elephants* by Tin San Bo

From the nightstand I take the elephant book and slip the picture of Ne Min and Myit Ko Naing between the pages. I clutch the book as if a part of Ne Min still lives within.

I place the book in my lap to flip through it, and I recognize some things Ne Min taught me. There's a picture of a man tending to an injured elephant, pouring what looks like sugar onto the wound. On another page, an elephant lies in a river while someone rubs its skin with a coconut husk. I can almost hear the rumbling purr of the elephant as the dust and dry skin are scrubbed away.

A herd surrounds a fallen elephant, some of them nudging it with their trunks.

On one of the last pages I see an elephant chained to a tree. The elephant looks larger than any others pictured in the book, but the chain that holds him is so thin it is almost lost in the grass. Why does such a strong elephant allow such a small chain to hold him? Doesn't he know he could break free if he tried? I run my hands over the rounded letters on the page and wish I knew what the words said. Those letters, written smoothly and with no sharp edges. Those words, that must say so much and hold such wisdom within their soft lines.

I hold Ne Min's hand once more. He finally looks like he is at peace, not holding on to the pain of elephants. He looks free, and I hope that he is.

I take the stone from my pocket and press it into Ne Min's hand. He is even more like this stone than I thought.

"This stone has quite a story." I don't know if Ne Min can hear me anymore, but I tell him about the stone anyway. About how it survived the weight and pressure bearing down on it, how it broke away and rolled far from home and spent many lifetimes knocked around by the river currents.

"This stone even passed through heat like fire," I tell him. "A weaker stone would have crumbled away into nothing."

I'll never know how the stone ever stopped tumbling and found its way out of the river. But I have to find my own way out of here. I wrap Ne Min's hand around the stone in his palm and let go.

I rush back to the stable and grab my bag. It holds my Ganesh figure, Nandita's carving, the empty iodine bottle, Ne Min's leaf, and the elephant box for Chanda. Nandita trumpets and swings her trunk back and forth. I think she knows that something important is happening.

As I place Ne Min's book in the bag, I stare at the marks I've carved. The lines I scratched with my pocket-knife each day make a long row across the stable wall. I unfold my knife and stab the point into the end of the row. My final mark.

Nandita follows me out of the stable, then bumps into me when the roar of Timir's truck freezes me in place. The cook shed blocks my view of the truck, so I can't see who is with him.

The engine quiets, and the wooden gate behind the cook shed creaks open, then closes. I peer around a tree and see three men following Timir to his office. One of them holds a large rifle.

Together Nandita and I run to the main gate. I find Sharad standing near the elephant truck.

"I am sorry about your father," I tell him.

He freezes, then turns away from the coil of rope he just loaded into the truck. His eyes narrow when he looks at me. "What are you talking about?"

"I know how much it hurts, losing your father. But it wasn't anyone's fault."

"You don't know—"

"—not even Anju's fault."

Sharad pounds the side of the truck with his fist so hard that I jump back from the noise.

"No, it was mine." He walks to the arena fence and leans on it. As he talks he stares at the ground. "I was the last one to close the lion cage that day. I thought I had locked it properly, but . . ."

We are both quiet for a long time. I wonder who Sharad has blamed more all these years, himself or the elephant. The pain on his face answers my question.

"It was an accident," I finally say. "And it was a long time ago. But did Anju's death help you feel any better? What would Nandita's death solve?"

"She could have killed me," he says.

"If she wanted to, she would have. And I could have left you on the ground and escaped, but I didn't. So now you can return the favor."

"What?"

"Give me the keys."

Sharad moves his hand to his key ring. His goodness has been buried for so long underneath so much anger, fear, and, I know now, guilt. I do not expect him to magically change, but if a bit of that goodness could dig its way out, just enough to help . . .

My hand in my pocket grips my knife. If I have to, I will slice open the pocket that holds Sharad's keys.

He stares at Nandita as she sways back and forth next to me.

I think I can win if he puts up a fight. He is still sore from Nandita's attack.

"This is a mistake," Sharad says. He pulls the keys from his pocket. "She is a wild animal, you know."

The hand on my knife relaxes. "I know, and she wants to go home."

He does not look at me as he asks, "How is Ne Min? I told Timir he needs a doctor. He doesn't want to get one, but maybe—"

When I don't answer he glances up at me. I shake my head to let him know it is too late for Ne Min.

Sharad sets the keys on a fence post and walks away.

I grab the keys and kneel next to Nandita. My hands shake as I slip the shackle key into the lock and turn it. The shackles clatter to the ground, followed by the chains around her neck and leg when I unlatch them.

As soon as I unlock and open the gate, Nandita runs through it and heads toward the forest that was once her home. She turns back to me and calls out a trumpet blast.

A hand grabs my shoulder.

"That animal is mine!" Timir yells. "Now go get her and bring her back, or you will never work off your debt to me."

I cannot move. But we have come so far, I can't let us fail now. If Nandita would just keep running, I could get myself out of here later. But she doesn't move either. Timir glances at her and says, "Fine. If you won't do the job yourself—" Only when he turns toward his office do I notice the workmen standing at the doorway. One of them holds the elephant gun. Timir waves him over. I back away from the fence.

"Take care of it now," he says as the man approaches.

Sharad runs to us, then leans on the fence while he catches his breath.

The workman raises the gun and aims it toward Nandita. My hand, so used to the comfort of the stone, reaches for my pocket before I realize the stone is no longer there. But I no longer need it. I know what to do. The same thing Nandita did for me when I faced danger.

I step in front of the barrel of the elephant gun. Standing here might not stop the man from firing, but it's the only chance I have now of saving Nandita.

The man moves aside and aims again. I follow.

"Fire!" Timir yells at the man.

Maybe this is where my story ends. I think of my village. I almost made it back. I think of my family, who will never know what happened to me. More than ever I hope that Chanda recovered from her illness, so Amma will not be alone.

"I can't," the man says. "The boy's in the way!"

"Just shoot him," says Timir.

The man steps aside and aims the gun. Again I follow, and stare into the blackness of the barrel.

He lowers the gun. "You hired me to shoot an elephant," he says to Timir. "I'm not shooting a boy, too."

Timir grabs the gun. "Then leave the job to someone who can do it." He hands the gun to Sharad. "Take care of it."

Sharad looks from the gun to Timir, then to me. He raises the gun. I place myself between him and Nandita.

This must be what Ne Min meant about being brave. Never in my life have I been so afraid, but here I stand.

We all jump at the rifle blast when Sharad fires—straight up into the sky. I look behind me to see Nandita galloping toward her forest home again. I know I should run, too, but my knees will give out under me if I move.

Nandita stops and turns back to us.

What is she doing? "Go on!" I yell as I wave her away. "Go home!"

But Nandita does not go. She kneels onto her front legs.

I turn back to Timir, and for the first time ever I look him right in the eyes. For all his yelling, for all his demands, he has never done anything. He might kill a mouse and never feel it, but he's afraid of anything that takes real work. He never lifted a shovel to dig Nandita's trap, never spent a moment training her, never even filled the trough or pitched hay. He is like a thundercloud that never produces rain. And he will not come after us.

"She has worked for you long enough," I say to him.

"And so have I. If you are so brave, go get her yourself. She won't be as gentle with you as she was with Sharad."

I run to Nandita, to take the last ride she will ever give.

Nandita heads to the forest with me on her back. I close my eyes to feel the wind on my face as she runs home. The wooden bell on her neck *clip-clops* along with her gallop. She trumpets and runs faster when we hear the answering calls of her herd. I lean forward and cling tighter to her neck so I will not fall off.

We pass the banyan tree where the trap used to be, and Nandita runs alongside the river, deeper into the forest. When we see the herd in the river, I reach up and pull myself onto a tree branch that Nandita passes under. Only then do I realize I still have Sharad's key ring. I laugh and toss it into the river. With no way to start the elephant truck and no way to lock the shackles, they will have a hard time catching a new elephant anytime soon.

The elephants trumpet and spin circles and touch Nandita with their trunks, celebrating even more excitedly than they did at the fence.

From a branch that hangs over the riverbank I watch Nandita standing in the river with the other elephants. Water splashes over her body, and she sprays her friend Indurekha with her trunk, just as she did when I first saw them last year.

For the rest of her days, when Nandita is hungry, she will eat. When she is thirsty, she will drink from the river.

She will walk without chains wherever she wants to go. When she is tired, she will rest. Someday she will be a mother—a good one, I know, a fierce protector of her children. Maybe one day she will be the leader of this herd.

I climb partway down the tree, then jump onto the riverbank. I'd like to give Nandita a proper goodbye, but I do not want to interrupt her homecoming.

From my bag, I grab Nandita's Ganesh carving, the one she still holds in her trunk sometimes while she sleeps. She probably doesn't need it anymore, but I place it on a low branch, just in case. Maybe when she sees it she will think of me.

I turn away to continue my journey to my own village. I don't know what I will find there. It might not look the same as I remember, but I am going home.

Water splashes and a branch snaps behind me. I do not turn around. For one last time, I will let Nandita sneak up on me.

When I feel her trunk on my shoulder, I turn around and act surprised to see her. She looks like she is laughing as she touches my head and face with her trunk. I step closer to give her a hug, and she places her trunk on my back. The rope that holds the wooden bell around her neck catches my eye. Why hadn't I heard the bell when she approached?

Both clappers still hang on either side of the bell, so it does not look to be broken. I grab the bell and shake it.

The sticks tap against the sides, but the *clip-clop-clip* I usually hear is gone. Mud drips onto my hand, and I turn the bell over to see more mud packed inside it.

Nandita has given me another gift from Ne Min. I laugh as I remember the story he told me while he was carving Nandita's bell.

"Some elephants, some of the smart ones, are mischievous. They clog their bell with mud to block its sound, if they wish to hide from you. Then you will have to search longer, but you will find her, and she will come to you."

I untie the rope from Nandita's neck. No one will need to look for her anymore. With the river water I clear the mud out of the bell, then pet Nandita's trunk once more. I will hang the bell outside my window, and when the wind blows, I'll think of Nandita and Ne Min.

Sometimes, I'm sure, I will wake up and look around for Nandita, or I'll smell breakfast and wonder what Ne Min is cooking. Then, as Ne Min said, the remembering will hit me with a pain that drops me to the ground. But I will stand up again. The sadness will be woven with a happiness that makes it worth feeling, and I will not run from it.

The river narrows, and I stop to rest on a moss-covered rock. I don't know how much farther the river will run, so I remove the empty iodine bottle from my bag. The chill of the riverbank seeps through the legs of my pants as I kneel to place the bottle in the water. I take time to enjoy the feel of the river current running over my hand. Before I return the bottle to my bag, I cap it tightly to hold in the last I will ever see of this river.

I move on toward my desert home, somewhere far ahead of me. Behind me, I hear a distant trumpeting in the forest, a joyful sound I have not heard from Nandita before. Finally, she is home.

It's been three days since I left the circus grounds. At times I've been able to catch a ride on the back of a grain truck to help me get to my village faster, but I've had to walk much of the way. One night a nice farmer let me stay at his house overnight so I wouldn't have to sleep outside. His family didn't have much to eat but they shared their dinner with me and refilled my bottle with water before I left.

Scatterings of thorny babul and kikar trees stand along the landscape now, instead of the towering forest trees that covered the road with a canopy of branches. I pass fields of chilies, the fruits turning orange and red. The roads I walk are no longer shaded, but that means I'm closer to home.

Last night I walked until I couldn't move anymore, then found a place to sleep under a roheda tree. My muscles groaned when I stood up this morning to continue my journey.

I've been walking all day long, but somehow the sun isn't going away. The bottle has been empty for a long time now, but I keep checking for one last drop. My exhausted body aches for rest after walking so far. How can I come this far just to fail, so close to home? But I see no water anywhere around me. I must try to keep walking and hope to find a drink somewhere. When I shove the bottle back into my bag, my hand brushes the wood of my Ganesh figure. I take it from the bag and hold it in my hand while I think about all I have been through since the day I carved it.

I've been separated from my family, never knowing if my sister survived or if her illness took her. I have seen a loved one hurt and another die. I have lived as a prisoner. And I broke free.

The journey ahead of me is still long, but whatever obstacles it holds, I know I've made it through far worse. I have to keep going.

I look to my right and notice something approaching in the distance. Too wide to be a person walking, but too slow to be a truck. As it gets closer I make out the curved horns and nodding heads of two bulls pulling a bullock cart.

The driver stops the cart next to me when I wave. In a scratchy voice I ask how far he's traveling. He will be passing by my village. The ride will be slow, but I will have a chance to rest. I climb onto the cart and sit atop the rice bags piled in the back. The driver hands me a jar of water, then snaps the reins of the bullocks to drive us forward.

In two gulps I drain the water jar. Even on the rough burlap of the rice bags, I fall asleep.

I wake when the driver calls to me. The cart has stopped. It doesn't seem like we could have ridden long enough to be near my home yet, but when I sit up the driver points toward my village. I thank the man as I hand him the empty water jar, then jump down from the cart to follow the sunset to my home.

I'd forgotten what it felt like to have sand in my shoes. Sand blows in my eyes, and I laugh. I cry when I see a camel.

When I reach the spot in the road where I last saw my mother, I stop. I look down the road that took me away, just as Amma did the day I left.

Baba said that a story is no good if you hear only the ending. You have to know how you got there. I still cannot say I will ever be thankful for much of what has happened to me, but everything I've ever done has brought me here.

A wagging tail catches my eye. I can't believe it.

"Raj?" I say. He trots over to me. I crouch down to pet him and laugh as he licks my face. He is fatter than I remember. So someone has been feeding him all this time.

The evening is cold, and the village stove pours smoke into the desert sky. I start to run to the courtyard, then stop when I see her carrying a basket of laundry to our house. Chanda pauses at our front door and drops the basket when she notices me.

Her smile is the same as our mother's. She looks tall. And healthy. I am so relieved to see her, I need all the strength I have left to keep from crumbling to the ground.

I wondered what I would say when I saw her again—if I saw her again—and if she would even recognize me, but we run to each other and crash into a hug as if no time or distance ever separated us. The pain of our separation fades as the scents of spices and bread dough in her clothes welcome me home.

We laugh when my stomach growls. I take my sister's hand and run toward the smell of baking rotis. Dinner is best when I pour the buttermilk while the roti is still hot.

AUTHOR'S NOTE

India has laws to protect elephants like Nandita and children like Hastin, but as everywhere in the world, there are people who ignore the law.

Since 1973, elephant capture in India has been illegal, except to relocate an elephant that has encroached upon land inhabited by people. For many years, circuses and zoos could legally obtain elephants that had been bred in captivity, but in 2009, a new law banned the use of elephants in Indian zoos and circuses. Many elephants already in zoos or circuses were transferred to national parks and animal sanctuaries. Concerns about the elephant population suffering because of poaching, habitat loss, and human-elephant conflicts led to later amendments to the Wildlife Protection Act, providing greater safeguards for elephants. Despite stricter regulations, forest departments in India continue to receive reports about illegal poaching and elephant trapping. Conservationists and animal welfare groups like the SPCA work to improve the lives of captive elephants in India and protect those in the wild.

Although child labor laws forbid the hiring of children, families who live in poverty often send their children to work in homes as servants or in factories. The children work long hours for very little pay and are sometimes abused by their employers. Laws banning child labor have been around since 1986, and in recent years new laws have been enacted to expand restrictions on hiring children. But millions of children still work under appalling conditions, and people who violate the law are seldom prosecuted.

Circuses were exempt from child labor laws until a 2010 amendment to the Child Labor Act banned circus owners from hiring children under the age of fourteen. Many owners ignored the ban, but in 2011 the Supreme Court in India ordered the government to enforce the ban by raiding circuses and rescuing child employees.

Advocacy groups in India are fighting vigilantly to end corruption so existing laws that protect the country's animals and children can be enforced.

ACKNOWLEDGMENTS

I feel like thanking everyone I've ever met or spoken to, but since acknowledgment pages tend to be more specific than that, special elephant-sized thanks go out to these people:

My agent, Joanna Stampfel-Volpe, equal parts cheerleader and ninja. Gina Loverde, who while interning at the agency was the first reader for *Chained* and the one to tell Joanna, "You have to read this." And the whole team at Nancy Coffey Literary and Media Representation: Nancy Coffey, Sara Kendall, Kathleen Ortiz, and Pouya Shahbazian.

Editor Margaret Ferguson, for believing in the story

and working countless hours to make it better. Assistant editor Susan Dobinick, copy editor Alicia Hudnett, and the marketing, publicity, sales, and design departments at Macmillan. Most people have no idea how much time and how many people it takes to bring a book to life. Thank you all for your dedication.

The Highlights Foundation for awarding the scholarship that allowed me to attend the Chautauqua Institute in 2008, where I learned how to be a better writer and met people I still call friends.

The community of writers I've met in person and online, for celebrating the good times, offering support through the not-so-good times, and keeping me entertained through it all.

Online critique group members who helped make the early chapters presentable: Gail Greenberg, Donna Grahmann, Kathy Hammer, Alicia Richardson, Charles Trevino, and Lisa Willis.

Those who critiqued the whole manuscript and celebrated with lunch and/or cake: Meet, Eat, & Critique members Mary David, Stephanie Green, Charles Trevino (who told me at the beginning, "This isn't a picture book, it's a novel"), and Brian C. Williams; Will Write For Cake members Laura Edge, Doris Fisher, Miriam King, Christina Mandelski, Monica Vavra, and Tammy Waldrop. I swear I'm not hanging out with you people just for the food.

The debut authors in the Apocalypsies and the Class

of 2k12 have made this journey a fun one to travel. Thank you for all the support and camaraderie as we flail along the road to publication together.

Stephanie Sheffield, who gave birth to Hastin by suggesting "How about adding a boy to take care of the elephant?" back when I thought I was only writing a little elephant book.

My family—those who were the first readers of Hastin's story, showed patience and understanding when I spent days in front of the computer in a Snuggie, and/or gave support and encouragement along the way.

Dr. Lynette Hart of the University of California at Davis for reviewing the manuscript and providing feedback about elephant behavior. Thank you for making sure those elephants were behaving themselves.

From the Houston Zoo: Daryl Hoffman, Curator of Large Mammals, Elephant Manager Martina Stevens, and all the elephant keepers, for information about elephant care and behavior during and after the zoo's Elephant Open House events.

Yale University's 2007 Burmese language study group led by Dr. U Khin Maung Gyi for coming up with name suggestions for Ne Min and his elephant. Viola L. Wu continued to answer my later questions about Burma and Burmese culture.

Journalist/researcher Surekha Sule for the information about rural housing in India, so I'd know what Hastin's house would look like.

Varsha Bajaj, Nandini Bajpai, Anjali Banerjee, and Mitali Perkins answered questions about India and Indian culture. Rani Iyer gave invaluable feedback after reading the full manuscript.

This book wouldn't be what it is without Uma Krishnaswami, who was as interested as I was in telling Hastin's story authentically. Thank you for all the hours spent reading the manuscript, the insightful comments about cultural accuracy and my writing, and answers to endless follow-up questions. I wish I could bottle your patience and wisdom and keep it at my desk. The story of Ganesh on page 147 is based on Uma Krishnaswami's retelling in *The Broken Tusk*.

The things I got right in this book are thanks to those who helped me along the way. Of course it would be impossible for anyone to teach me everything I needed to know, so if I got anything wrong it's because I didn't ask the right questions.

Thanks, everyone, for helping me get here.